'What you're say_ _ _ grandmother y_ _ _ to me?'

'Kirst, Gran's ill. She wants to see me settled. I told her a white lie, that's all.'

Kirsty snorted. 'White lie? I think it's a bit more than that.'

He shrugged. 'I told her I'd met someone special, just to keep her happy. But she leapt to conclusions and thought I meant you. The longer it went on, the more elaborate the lies got—and the next thing I knew I'd told her we were engaged!'

'Ben, have you considered that she might have angina, and that's all? You're a registrar in A and E—you see cases like that all the time. If she was seriously ill she'd tell you.'

'All I want to do is make Gran happy. If it is more than angina, I don't want her thinking I'm still drifting around. I'm asking you to do me a favour. Will you come with me to visit my grandmother as my fiancée?'

A&E DRAMA

Blood pressure is high and pulses are racing in these fast-paced, dramatic stories from Mills & Boon® Medical Romance™. They'll bust a gut to save a life in an emergency, be they a crash team, ER doctors, fire, air and land rescue or paramedics. There are lots of critical engagements amongst the high tensions and emotional passions in these exciting stories of lives and loves at risk!

A&E DRAMA
Hearts are racing!

Kate Hardy lives on the outskirts of Norwich with her husband, two small children, two lazy spaniels—and too many books to count! She wrote her first book at age six when her parents gave her a typewriter for her birthday. She had the first of a series of sexy romances published at age 25, and swapped a job in marketing communications for freelance health journalism when her son was born so she could spend more time with him. She's wanted to write for Mills & Boon since she was twelve—and when she was pregnant with her daughter, her husband pointed out that writing Medical Romances would be the perfect way to combine her interest in health issues with her love of good stories. It really is the best of both worlds—especially as she gets to meet a new gorgeous hero every time…

HIS EMERGENCY
FIANCÉE

BY
KATE HARDY

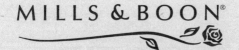

In proud and loving memory of Sandra Christine
Shirley Sewell, 1945–1986
—the best mother, the best nurse and a true inspiration

*First published in Great Britain 2003
Harlequin Mills & Boon Limited,
Eton House, 18-24 Paradise Road, Richmond, Surrey TW9 1SR*

© *Pamela Brooks 2003*

ISBN 0 263 83441 7

*Set in Times Roman 10½ on 11 pt.
03-0403-50382*

*Printed and bound in Spain
by Litografía Rosés, S.A., Barcelona*

CHAPTER ONE

BEN stared at the letter in dismay. No. He couldn't have read it right. He scanned it again—and then for a third time.

No, there was no mistake.

He closed his eyes. Kirsty was going to kill him. She'd never agree to help, not with this.

She was his only hope of getting out of this mess, so he'd have to pull out the stops. All of them. Thankfully, he was off duty today.

He picked up the phone, dialled a familiar number and crossed his fingers that one of the more sympathetic nurses on the surgical ward would answer.

Kirsty eased her shoulders as she walked down the path. Right now, all she wanted to do was have a long, deep bath, then sink in front of the sofa with some cheese on toast and an old film. Though, no doubt, Ben had already gone out, leaving the kitchen covered in crumbs, so she'd have to clear away all his mess before she could even fix herself some food. Not to mention clearing his papers from the table before she could sit down to eat.

Maybe it was time she sat down with him and hammered out a few ground rules. 'Bit late after all these years, Kirst,' she told herself wryly. Ben's habits were firmly entrenched. 'And that's the first step to madness, talking to yourself,' she added. 'What you need is a cat.' Though Ben wasn't the real reason she was angry. That dubious honour belonged to her new boss, Guy Chambers. On second thoughts, she didn't need a cat: a dog would be better. One with big teeth. And she could send him in the direction of her boss's rear and see how *he* liked being nipped…

She unlocked the front door and stopped dead. There was music from the kitchen—so the light in the living room wasn't just their mutually agreed burglar deterrent. Ben was home. Which meant he was entertaining.

She closed her eyes. That was all she needed—having to be polite to one of Ben's women. Kirsty hadn't met her but she already knew what the woman would be like—what *all* Ben's women were like. Six inches taller than Kirsty's five feet four, half a stone lighter, long blonde or red hair instead of short mouse brown, and big china-blue eyes instead of ordinary brown. Not to mention drop-dead gorgeous instead of plain and little.

Lucky that she was an expert at smash-and-grab. Into kitchen, make sandwich, smile politely, grab orange juice and choc bar from fridge, head for bathroom and long, long soak in bath. She could do it in two minutes flat.

She dropped her bag at the foot of the stairs and sidled to the kitchen. She couldn't hear Ben talking to anyone. Hopefully that didn't mean he was locked in a smooch. She rolled her eyes. She had to be the only female under seventy-five in the hospital who hadn't fallen for Dr Charming. Ben had dark hair with a slight wave in it, huge cornflower blue eyes with unfairly long lashes contrasting sharply with his pale skin, fabulous bone structure and a megawatt smile. He could have been a TV doctor with those looks.

And he also happened to be her best friend as well as her housemate. So even if she hadn't been so far out of his league in the looks department, he'd be off limits on two more counts. Besides, she didn't think of him in *that* way. He was just Ben.

Steeling herself, she sauntered into the kitchen—and stopped dead. It *looked* as if he was entertaining. Every surface gleamed, there was no clutter—probably all stashed under his bed and it'd be back in the morning—

a Bach cello suite was playing softly, something smelt gorgeous enough to make her stomach rumble and Ben was sitting at the table set for two.

But there was no stunning blonde or redhead opposite him.

Maybe she'd gone to the bathroom.

'Hi, Ben. I'll be out of your way in two minutes,' she said brightly.

'Don't be daft.' He smiled at her. 'Sit.'

'I've had a hell of a day. I'm not up to socialising,' she warned.

'You don't have to socialise with anyone, Kirst,' he told her soothingly.

That *voice*. Like warm velvet, with just the hint of a Scots burr when he rolled his 'r's. Especially when it was accompanied by the smile that made you feel you were the most important person in the world. No wonder even the most difficult patient melted at Ben Robertson's bedside manner. 'But you've got someone round, haven't you?' She gestured to the table.

'Actually, Kirst, I'm cooking for you.'

Her eyes narrowed. 'Did you forget to pay the electricity bill or something?'

He laughed. 'You're such a cynic.'

'No, I've known you since our first week at university,' she retorted. They'd hit it off so well that when they'd ended up training in the same south coast hospital they'd agreed to share a house. She put up with the constant stream of Ben's girlfriends, and he made sure she didn't spend all her time at her books. The arrangement worked perfectly.

But it didn't include Ben cooking her posh dinners.

What was he up to? A nasty thought made her stomach feel like lead. He wasn't going to tell her he was moving out and getting married, was he? No, of course not. Ben's women never lasted more than three dates—even the really nice ones. He couldn't handle commitment.

Or had he met the right one at last?

She didn't want to think about that. The way her job was shaping up was bad enough. For her home life to fall to pieces, too, was more than she could handle right now.

'Kirst, you said yourself you've had a bad day. Sit down.' He gave her a searching look. 'Are you on call now?'

'No.' And the more time that passed without her seeing Guy Chambers, the better. If she could prevent any RTAs in a twenty-mile radius by sheer will-power, Southbay would have the lowest accident statistics ever for the next twenty years.

Something must have shown on her face because Ben looked, well, almost *nervous*, she thought. 'It's all right. I'm not going to savage *you*.'

'Good.' He poured her a glass of wine. 'Have a swig of this, then.'

She took a sip and closed her eyes. 'Mmm. New World Merlot, unless I'm mistaken.'

'Correct, Dr Brown.' He smiled. 'Give me three minutes and I'll feed you.'

Kirsty watched him as he pulled the casserole dish out of the oven and ladled the contents onto two plates, added two jacket potatoes and a dollop of sour cream, sprinkled some chopped fresh parsley over the top, then pulled a bag of ready-prepared veg from the microwave, slit the bag and heaped them next to the potatoes.

It smelt good and it tasted even better. Particularly as she hadn't had to cook it after a hard day at Jimmy's, as all the staff called St James's Hospital in Southbay. 'Ben, this is fabulous. Thanks.'

'Any time.' He looked at her. 'What's happened?'

'Nothing,' she grumped, her mood deflating instantly as she thought about work. Work, and Guy Chambers.

'Patient or colleague?'

'Stop nagging, Robertson.'

He gave her his most charming smile. 'OK. Eat first, then tell me.'

She gave a noncommittal murmur and continued eating.

Ben ate in silence, too, though he was feeling more and more edgy about what he had to tell her. Something had obviously gone badly wrong at work today and he had a nasty feeling his news was going to light the touch-paper. Something or someone had got under her skin and Kirsty hardly ever got rattled. She was plain-speaking, yes— what you saw was definitely what you got—but she was nice with it. She never really lost her temper.

Not even when it was deserved, he thought with a flash of guilt. He was one of the worst when it came to taking advantage of her good nature. When this was all over, he'd keep her in fresh roses and best Belgian chocolate for a *year*, he decided.

If she was still speaking to him.

He topped up her glass without comment, then took a tub of her favourite ice cream from the freezer, scooped out a huge bowlful, added the cannoli wafers he'd bought specially for her and presented the bowl with a bow.

Again, suspicion flashed over her face. 'Whatever you've done, Ben, you might as well tell me n—'

'Later,' he broke in. 'Tell me about your day first.' And then he might chicken out of asking her. Maybe he could talk someone else into pretending to be Kirsty…

Though that wouldn't work either. His grandmother already knew what Kirsty looked like. 'Big list, was it?' he asked.

'Well, your lot kept us busy. An emergency appendix we caught just before it ruptured and one RTA with a punctured lung and more leaks than a colander.' She ticked them off on her fingers. 'One set of varicose veins to strip out. One patient booked in for a bypass who swears blind he's given up smoking, even though you can smell it on his clothes and see the yellow stains on his fingers. And I know damned well he hasn't listened to a

word I've said and he's going to go straight back to drinking too much, eating way too much saturated fat, smoking
and taking no exercise. Another to sweet-talk into staying
put for her bypass tomorrow because she's terrified of
going under the knife. A ton of paperwork. Oh, and meeting my new boss, Guy Chambers.'

The orange sparks in her eyes told him all he needed
to know. Guy Chambers was the reason she was simmer-
ing. 'Tony's replacement?'

'Tony's replacement,' she confirmed grimly.

'What's the problem?'

'Let's just say we're not going to be each other's favourite person.'

'What's so bad about him? I was in Resus when he did
the rounds to meet everyone so I haven't actually talked
to him, but he's got a good reputation.'

'Ben, he's a…he's a…' She scowled. 'Well, if that's
what being a top surgeon does to you, I'm changing spe-
cialties. Starting tomorrow morning.'

His hands balled immediately into fists. 'What's he
done to you, Kirst?'

She gave him an old-fashioned look. 'I can handle it.'

'I know.' With three older brothers, Kirsty was more
than able to stand up for herself. He knew that. Oddly, it
didn't stop him wanting to protect her.

She grimaced. 'My bum's probably not as blue as the
scrub nurse's.'

'Just give him one of your looks.'

'Mmm.'

He'd bet she'd already done that. Probably said something, too. And if Guy Chambers had the kind of ego that
went with bum-pinching, Kirsty had just shot herself in
the foot where her career was concerned, because he
wouldn't give her a decent reference when a consultancy
came up. Nothing she could argue with, of course—it'd
be what he *didn't* say that would do the most damage.

'Kirst, be careful. It's not a good idea to, well, make an enemy of someone like him so quickly.'

'Play up and play the game, you mean?' She shook her head. 'He might just as well come out with it and say women shouldn't be surgeons. After all, you need a bit of brute strength as well as skill with a needle, and we *delicate* little flowers…'

'Come on, Kirst. Tony always said you had the makings of a brilliant surgeon, and he should know. He taught you.'

Kirsty crunched into one of the wafers, savouring the richness of the chocolate and hazelnut filling. 'And Tony's on indefinite sick leave, so what he thinks doesn't count any more.' Her eyes narrowed. 'So, make my day complete. What have you done?'

'Um…' Now definitely wasn't the right time to ask her.

'Ben?' It was more of a warning than a question.

'I need a favour, Kirst. A big one.' Sighing, he stood up, retrieved the letter from the kitchen drawer and passed it across to her.

She glanced at the opening and frowned. 'It's to you. From your gran.'

He nodded. 'Read it.'

She did, and her mouth grew tighter and tighter. When she'd finished, she stared at him. 'Explain. And it had better be good.'

Worse than lit touch-paper. Her voice was very, very quiet. Which meant that Kirsty was absolutely furious. He'd only seen her this angry once before, when they'd been students, and she'd always refused to tell him what had happened.

'Gran's poorly,' he said heavily.

She folded her arms and looked him straight in the eye. 'Define poorly.'

'She says it's angina but…' He shook his head. 'You know Gran. She gets the flu and says it's a slight sniffle. If she's admitting to angina…' His voice faded. If his grandmother admitted to that much, what *wasn't* she admitting to? He'd been asking himself that ever since she'd told him, and the more he thought about it the scarier the possibilities were.

'Have you spoken to her doctor?'

He shook his head. 'No point, is there? Patient confidentiality—he won't tell me a thing unless Gran gives him written permission, and she's hardly likely to do that if she wants to keep this from me.'

There were more orange sparks in her brown eyes—so Kirsty clearly wasn't convinced. 'What you're saying is, on the strength of something you haven't even confirmed, you told Morag you're engaged…to me?'

'It wasn't like that.'

'Then how was it?' Her voice was still dangerously quiet.

'Kirst, she's the only family I've got.' Not *strictly* true, but Morag was the only one who counted. Ben's father had died when he was four and his mother had gone to pieces. Morag Robertson had been his rock then—and a year or so later, when his mother had found someone else, a man who hadn't wanted a small child around to complicate things, and sent Ben to live with Morag. And later still, when he'd been in his teens and his mother had talked about him coming to live with her again, following her divorce. Until she'd found another man to run to three weeks later and had changed her mind again.

'Ben, why did you tell her you were engaged to me?'

He sighed. 'It was a mistake.'

'You can say that again!'

'Kirst, she'd been on at me to settle down.'

'And break the hearts of all the single women—and probably half the married ones, too—at Jimmy's?'

'Ha, ha.' He scowled. 'Kirst, Gran's old and she's ill. She wants to see me settled. I told her a white lie, that's all.'

Kirsty snorted. 'White lie? I think it's a *bit* more than that.'

'I told her I'd met someone special.' He shrugged. 'I just made her up to keep Gran happy. But she leapt to conclusions and thought I meant you. I didn't have the heart to explain, so I let her go on thinking it. I didn't think it'd do any harm.' He rubbed a hand across his eyes. 'I had no idea it was going to go this far. The longer it went on, the more elaborate the lies got...and the next thing I knew, I'd told her we were getting engaged.'

Kirsty frowned. 'I talked to her on the phone only last week and she didn't breathe a word to me about it.'

He flushed. 'I...um...said you were a bit shy about it. About us being friends for so long and not, you know... Anyway, she said she was happy to wait for you to tell her all about it and she wouldn't dream of embarrassing you by bringing it up until you were ready to talk about it.'

'You *devious*... Words fail me!' she growled at him. 'You've got to tell her the truth.'

'She's ill.'

'Ben, have you ever considered that she might have angina, and that's all? You're a registrar in A and E— you see cases like that all the time, and you did a rotation on the geriatric ward. She knows you'd realise she had a problem and you'd guess exactly what it was, so she told you about it to stop you thinking the worst. If she was seriously ill, she'd tell you.'

'Would she?'

Kirsty rolled her eyes. 'Be sensible. Of course she would. And you know people can live for years with angina. To listen to Morag, you'd never think she was well into in her seventies. She's on every committee going in the village and she told me she's doing a course in website design next term.'

'You know Gran. She's always done six things at once. But she's never pressured me about settling down before—I think this is her way of telling me she's…' He broke off, unable to voice his fears. Speaking them aloud would make them more real. Would make them *happen*.

He was as bad as Luke. It hit her like a physical pain. Ben—the one man she thought she could trust—was a liar. She gritted her teeth. She'd always thought Ben was honest. He made it clear to his girlfriends right at the start that he wasn't in the market for commitment, just for fun. But at heart he was just like Luke, her ex-boyfriend. Lying, to get his own way. The words echoed down the years to her, still searing her heart as much as the day she'd overheard them: 'The betting's odds on…' She'd thought it was so special, and it had all been a lie.

Just like Ben was lying now. Anger burned in Kirsty's voice. 'You lied to her.'

'Yes—no—Kirst, I can't think straight. All I want is to make Gran happy. If it *is* more than angina… I don't want her to die, thinking I'm still drifting around.'

'Still playing at Dr Charming, you mean?' The words came out before she could stop them—or dull the biting edge to her voice.

He flushed. 'I just like making people happy, Kirst. And, let's face it, most of the people in A and E don't have any reason to smile. If a bit of banter makes it easier to deal with what's happening to them, that's fine by me.'

'I'm not talking about banter. I'm talking about *lying*.'

He raked a hand through his hair. 'Does it have to be a lie?'

Her mouth dropped open. 'Are you asking me to—to…?' To marry him?

'I'm asking you to do me a favour. Will you come to Scotland with me for a weekend as my fiancée?'

'You're asking me to lie.'

'I'm asking you to make an old woman happy.'

Her mouth tightened. 'And just supposing I'm already engaged to someone else?'

'Kirst, you haven't even *dated* anyone in six months.'

The next thing she knew, Ben was sitting down, looking shocked, with a red handprint across his face. *Her* handprint. She swallowed. 'I'm sorry.'

He rubbed his face. 'No, I'm sorry. I deserved that. Though I wasn't implying you're unattractive, Kirst. Of course you're not.'

'No.' Her voice was dry. She was plain little Kirsty Brown, and she knew it. So did everyone else. Wasn't that one of the reasons why Luke—? No, she wasn't going to think about that now.

'You're working long hours and spending all your spare time studying, that's all I meant. And if anyone asks you out you always turn them down. Even I have a hard job dragging you down the pub or the Chinese, and I'm your best friend.'

'Yes.' She bit her lip as guilt flooded through her. Ben wasn't the one she wanted to slap. But slapping her boss or kneeing him where it hurt wasn't going to help her career. 'I'm sorry.'

'Me, too.'

They stared at each other for a long moment.

'So. What now?' he asked.

'You *lied*, Ben.'

'With good intentions,' he reminded her. 'All I'm asking is that you'll be my fiancée for the weekend.'

'Fake fiancée,' she reminded him. 'No.'

He looked at her. 'Tell me, did Chambers try it on with all the female staff, or just the unattached ones?'

Kirsty thought about it. 'The unattached ones,' she said finally.

'There's your answer, then. If you're my fiancée, he'll leave you alone.'

'Ben, I am not getting engaged to you.'

'What's wrong with me?' He pantomimed hurt.

'Want a list?' She rubbed her hands together. 'You

never clean the bath. You leave wet towels everywhere. You're untidy. You've—'

'Shared a house with you for the best part of nine years,' he pointed out, 'since our second year as med students. So I can't be *that* bad.'

'Don't fish.' She glowered at him.

Ben poured her another glass of wine. 'Our engagement could be the best thing that's ever happened to both of us.'

'How do you make that out?'

He shrugged. 'It's obvious. Gran'll think I'm settled and she'll be happy, and Guy Chambers'll think you're unavailable so he'll leave you alone.'

'More like, he'll decide that if I'm engaged there's no point in me taking any more exams because I'll be off to have hundreds of kids as soon as I get married,' she said glumly.

'When he's had a chance to see your work, he'll know how good you are and he'll know you're headed for the top,' Ben countered.

'Even so. Nothing's going to help the Guy Chambers situation.'

'This might.'

'Yeah, right. And then I'll have every female in the hospital looking daggers at me for wearing your ring.' She sighed. 'Why can't you ask one of them?'

'Because Gran knows you. She likes you, Kirst. She trusts you.'

'Read my lips. I am not getting engaged to you.'

'Just until things settle down.'

'No.'

'Please?'

The way he batted his eyelashes at her forced a grin to her lips. Honestly. Charming didn't go anywhere near enough to describe him. Nearly everyone she knew was like putty in his hands. She knew his faults better than anyone—and he could still sweet-talk her, most of the time. 'I'll think about it,' she said grudgingly.

He reached over and hugged her. 'Thanks, Kirst. I knew I could rely on you.'

Rely on her. Plain, reliable Kirsty Brown. The words rankled. 'I *said* I'd think about it. That's not a yes,' she warned. Sometimes, she dreamed about dyeing her hair blonde, wearing skirts that were way too short with heels almost too high to walk on, wearing lots of slut-red lipstick and being late for absolutely everything... But that wasn't her. Kirsty was the one people always rang when they needed help. She was the youngest of four but she'd somehow stepped into the role of being the sensible grown-up one, always getting her brothers out of scrapes and making sure they remembered everyone's birthdays. That was probably why she'd put up with Ben for so long. And it'd stay that way until Ben found the love of his life and settled down in a country cottage with roses round the door and three perfect children, while she remained firmly superglued to the shelf.

Ben was smiling again. The megawatt smile. The smile that made every other female under the age of seventy faint. The smile to which Kirsty was immune.

'OK. No pressure. I'll ask you again on Thursday.'

He was giving her *two days* to think about it? And that wasn't pressure? 'Ben Robertson, you're in a league of your own,' she said. And she wasn't in it. Which made her answer on Thursday obvious...didn't it?

CHAPTER TWO

THE next morning, they were both on early shift and they walked into Jimmy's together. To Kirsty's intense relief, Ben didn't mention anything about their pretend engagement. Maybe he'd thought about it and seen sense. On the other hand, she knew she'd better have some good arguments up her sleeve. When Ben had his heart set on something, he usually got it. And where his grandmother was concerned, he'd spare no effort.

They parted at the entrance, Ben off to the medical assessment unit where he was rostered until the end of the week, and Kirsty to the surgical ward to do a quick round before scrubbing up for her list. Mrs Morgan was still nervous about her bypass, and Kirsty sat on the edge of her bed, holding her hand. 'I know it's scary, having an operation, but it's the best thing for you. You'll feel so much better afterwards,' she said softly, 'that it's worth a bit of nervousness now.'

Mrs Morgan gave a watery smile. 'I know I'm just being silly.'

'It's a big step. It's only natural to feel worried about it,' Kirsty reassured her. 'Are there any questions you'd like to ask me?'

She shook her head.

'Mr Morgan?'

The pale-faced man sitting on the chair next his wife's bed smiled at her. 'No, love. You went through it all yesterday—what you're going to do and what's going to happen afterwards.'

'And you're happy you know what to expect? I can go through it again, if it helps,' Kirsty offered.

'Would you? I—I just can't remember what you said.' Mrs Morgan bit her lip.

'It's a lot to take in,' Kirsty said with a smile. 'When you come round, you'll have a tube down your throat— what we call an endotracheal tube—for a few hours. It's routine after an operation like this to make sure your tongue doesn't block your airways and it helps you breathe. It means you won't be able to speak, so we'll have a pad and pencil at the ready so you can still tell us if there's anything you need. Your mouth will probably feel a bit dry so the nurses will keep cleaning it for you to make sure you're comfortable. There'll be a drain in your chest—that just takes all the unnecessary fluid off and the nurses can check everything's as it should be— but it'll be covered by a dressing at first. You'll have what we call an arterial line in for the first day, so we can check your heart rate and rhythm. We also need to check you're not retaining fluid, so we'll need to measure what goes in and out—that means you'll be on a drip and a catheter.' She smiled gently. 'I know that all sounds horrible but it won't be for long—and you won't feel like dragging yourself out of bed to go to the loo anyway, on the first day. By day two, you should be on your feet, and you'll probably be home within a week.'

'Home.' Mrs Morgan's face creased with longing.

'Hey, you'll be fine. You've got me looking after you.' Kirsty squeezed her hand. 'I'll see you in Theatre.' She winked. 'Don't you go getting into mischief on the way.'

Mrs Morgan managed a weak smile and Kirsty left the ward to get changed for Theatre. Guy Chambers was already scrubbed up, his fair curly hair hidden under a surgical turban. Paul Fisher, the SHO, was also ready. Neither of them smiled at her entrance. Kirsty said nothing but changed and scrubbed swiftly. In the old days, Tony and Paul would have teased her for being late and claimed she was chatting up the patients—but now Tony was gone and Paul had turned unnaturally serious. Surely the consultant wasn't still sulking because she'd asked him not to touch her backside again? Kirsty was tempted to ask Paul privately what he thought of Chambers, but decided against it. There was no point in inflaming the situation further. She had to face facts: their firm had changed, and she just had to put up with it. Put up and shut up.

She walked into Theatre—and even that had changed. Tony always operated to some kind of cello music and she'd grown to like it. With Chambers, everything was in deadly silence. She suppressed a sigh. At least when she'd made the first incision she could concentrate on her job.

But she was denied even that satisfaction. Chambers, instead of asking either of his juniors if they wanted to lead, decided to do it himself and barked the occasional order at Paul.

Should she mention that she'd already done half a dozen bypasses on her own, with Tony acting as her back-up? No. He'd think she was showing off and give her another black mark. Ask him if she could do it? He'd probably take great delight in saying no. Her lips tightened behind her mask, and she did what was so obviously expected of her: she observed.

Give him the benefit of the doubt, she told herself. It was his first week here. He didn't know her or Paul and he probably hadn't had time to read any staff files and find out what they'd already done. He was just playing it safe.

But a little voice in her head told her she was kidding herself. Chambers had an axe to grind—but why? She didn't usually have major personality clashes with people she worked with—nurses, auxiliaries, junior doctors or seniors. Not even the most dragon-like secretary. In fact, Chambers was the first.

He threw the odd question at her during the operation but most of them were directed at Paul. She didn't quite understand why—did he think that she, as the surgical reg, should already know the answers? But if that was the case, that begged the question why he hadn't let her operate under his supervision.

Don't let him rile you, she warned herself. That's probably what he wants. An outburst from you and he'll claim you're hormonal and not suited to the job.

She kept her temper—just—at his next words.

'Fisher—close for me.'

If he'd swept off then, Kirsty would have been happy enough to supervise Paul. But no. He did it himself. As if he didn't trust her to do it properly.

What was the point in me even being here? she thought. Crossly, she changed out of scrubs and went back down to the ward.

'Has Mr Chambers seen Mr Morgan yet?' she asked Jenny, the ward sister.

Jenny shook her head. 'He said you'd do it.'

That figures, Kirsty thought. He's not a people person, and I am. 'Fine.' She forced a smile to her face. 'I'll go and have a chat.'

'Kirst, are you OK?'

'Never better,' Kirsty said lightly. Jenny was a good friend, but Kirsty wasn't going to take any risks. If she said what she thought about Chambers, it would be just her luck that the man would creep up on her and overhear her. 'I'll see Mr Morgan, then I'll take my break.' Lunch with Ben. That was what she needed to cheer her up. 'Bleep me if you need me.'

Mr Morgan was delighted to see her. 'My Elsie's all right, then?'

'It's early days, but we're not expecting any problems. Everything went according to plan,' Kirsty reassured him.

'I knew she'd be safe in your hands, lass.'

Kirsty made herself smile back. 'Better than that. Mr Chambers did the operation,' she said. 'Now, if you've any questions, just ask—that's what we're here for.' She looked at the whiteboard above the bed. 'Definitely the best care here—she's under Jenny. That's the bossy one in the dark blue uniform,' she added in a stage whisper as Jenny walked into the room.

'Bossy, yourself,' Jenny retorted with a grin.

Kirsty wrinkled her nose, left her to it and went down to the medical assessment unit. 'Ben around?' she asked Sarah, the triage nurse.

'Just follow the line of swooning women,' Sarah told her, laughing.

Kirsty chuckled. 'Business as usual, then?'

'What is?' said Ben, emerging from behind a curtain. 'Hello, Kirst. I wasn't expecting to see you.'

'Got time for some lunch?'

He looked at her, clearly cottoning onto the situation straight away—Kirsty needed to take her mind off work. He turned to Sarah. 'What's the patient situation?'

'Grab the chance while you can,' Sarah said. 'I'll probably have to bleep you halfway through your sandwich.'

'You know where I'll be,' he said. 'Come on, you. Lunch is my shout. Soggy tuna or dried-up grated cheese?' He draped his arm loosely round Kirsty's shoulders and shepherded her out of the department.

Even when they were out in the corridor, he left his arm where it was. 'Bad morning?'

'Yup. I'll talk later, but just distract me for now before I misuse my scalpel.'

He gave a low whistle. 'OK. Distraction. How about a second opinion on a case?'

'Want to go back?'

'When soggy tuna calls?' he teased. 'Anyway, my patient—seventeen, enlarged liver, aggressive and a ton of acne. Renal pain but not admitting to much. Pale skin, dark shadows under the eyes. I've ordered liver-function tests, urine sample and CDT—though he didn't smell of alcohol.' CDT or carbohydrate-deficient transferrin tests checked for alcohol abuse. The transferrin molecules, responsible for transporting iron around the body, were found in high concentration in the liver; in cases of alcohol abuse they became deficient in carbohydrates.

'Enlarged liver, renal pain.' Kirsty thought about it. 'Could be hepatitis. Is he a user?'

'Says not.' Ben shrugged. 'No track marks. And he's apparently got a hundred per cent attendance record at school, so it's not that likely.'

'Sex?' She wrinkled her nose. 'No, he's too young to be that promiscuous.'

'It only takes one partner,' Ben said, following her train of thought.

'I'll take a look at him, if you like.'

'After lunch,' Ben said firmly, steering her into the canteen.

She scanned the room quickly. No sign of Chambers. Hopefully he wouldn't follow Tony's precedent and eat with the lesser mortals in the staff canteen—which meant she could have her lunch in peace.

The tuna sandwiches were as soggy as Ben had suggested, but Kirsty knew from long experience they were better than the grated cheese which leaked like sawdust onto your plate. And Sarah's predictions were wrong for once—they managed to eat their sandwiches and grab a latte without being bleeped.

'Got time to see my distraction, then?' Ben asked.

Kirsty glanced at her watch. 'Plenty.'

She accompanied him back to the MAU and Ben introduced her to his patient.

'Adam, this is Kirsty. She's come to have a quick look at you.'

The seventeen-year-old grunted in response.

'Do you mind if I examine you?' Kirsty asked.

He answered with a shrug which she took for consent and gently examined him, noting his wince as she touched the area around his liver.

'We haven't managed to get in contact with your dad yet. Do you have a number for your mother?' Ben asked.

'No.'

The curtain swished aside. 'Ben, sorry to interrupt—I need your advice for a moment,' Sarah said, the calmness of her voice belying the trace of panic in her eyes.

'I'll be back in a minute,' Ben promised.

Kirsty studied the boy. He didn't look the type to use drugs…and yet something clicked in the back of her mind. Something about the way he looked—and hadn't Ben said something about aggressiveness? Extra testosterone—that would explain the acne, too. She glanced at the textbook he'd been studying. 'Physics. You're doing your A levels?'

'What of it?'

'It was my favourite subject. I almost did astrophysics for my degree,' she said. 'I fancied being a rocket scientist.'

'So why didn't you? 'Cos you're a girl?'

'Nope. Because I like people—and rocket science is a bit too lonely for me.' She looked levelly at him. This was a huge risk and if she was wrong, she'd have more than just apologies to make. But the tone of his voice made her think it was too much of a coincidence. 'Is that what they're telling you?'

'What?'

'At school. That you're too much of a girl?'

Pain flashed across his face, quickly masked. 'That's what you think, too.'

She shook her head. 'Not at all. But let me tell you one thing. Bullies always lose. Always.'

'How would you know?' he asked bitterly. 'Did they all tell you your mum's a whore and she's run off with the milkman because she's already been through six postmen?'

So that was why he didn't have a number for his mum. She'd left. The chances were, Ben's father was still licking his own wounds and hadn't noticed how unhappy his son was, or just couldn't cope with anything more. 'No.

It was something…more personal.' She dragged in a deep breath. Even thinking of the way Luke had betrayed her with his cronies, had used her and laughed at her, still made her feel vulnerable and angry and hurt all at the same time. 'But the people who bullied me flunked their exams and were thrown out. I came out top of the class and I'm doing a job I love. So who gets the last laugh?'

He stared at her in silence.

She tried again. 'You're top of the class—yes?'

He nodded.

'And they're—what, bottom?'

'One of them's already dropped out,' he admitted.

'They're jealous of you. That's why they're calling you names.' She looked at the dull yellow bruising on his side. 'And getting physical. Because they feel insecure and it's all they know how to do. You're going to the gym, right?'

He flushed. 'Training seven days a week.'

'With steroids.'

He flinched but said nothing.

'I take it you're not doing biology?'

He shook his head. 'Maths, further maths and chemistry.'

'Pity,' she said, 'because if you'd been doing biology you'd know what steroid abuse does to your body. It can affect your heart, your liver—and your fertility. So what seems like the right solution now is going to do you an awful lot more harm in the long run—and you can't use weight training against a gang of people.'

'So what *do* I do, then? If I tell someone about them, they'll just wait for me until they get me without anyone seeing and really do me over. Maybe with knives next time.'

'Try martial arts,' she said.

'Kung fu? Come on. That's not going to stop them.'

'Isn't it? Most of the martial arts are based on protecting yourself. That's all you need—technique and brains win over brawn any time.'

'Do they?'

'Trust me. I'm a doctor,' she deadpanned.

For the first time, she saw him smile. 'That's a terrible line.'

'I know, but it's true.' She took his hand. 'Adam, throw the steroids away. You don't need them to combat violence. It's *technique* you need. Try the community relations officers at the police station—they're bound to know some self-defence classes locally. They'll point you in the right direction. Or look on the notice-board in the gym you go to. Something's bound to be advertised.'

'And this?' Adam pointed to his liver.

'The pain will go away. But if you continue abusing steroids, it'll get worse. Plus, your heart'll start to play up and you can kiss goodbye to the idea of having kids in ten years' time or whatever.' She ticked off the minuses on her fingers. 'Is it worth letting them do that to you?'

He was silent.

'Adam?' she prompted gently.

'No,' he admitted in a near-whisper.

'Then promise me you'll try another way.' She smiled. 'A few years down the line, you'll be famous and raking it in, and they'll be stuck in dead-end jobs. Trust me.'

'That's what happened to you?'

'Something like that.' After that terrible day when she'd found out the truth about Luke, that his relationship with her had all been a big joke at her expense and his friends had been running a book on how long it'd take him to get her knickers off, she'd avoided him. She had no idea what had happened to him. His friends had dropped out and he'd left. Knowing Luke, he'd probably used his parents' money to smooth the path to a retake at another university. 'Trust me. Bullies never win.'

'Dr Brown, I hate to break up such a touching scene, but I've been trying to track you down,' a voice drawled. 'Or have you forgotten this afternoon's list?'

'Sounds like I gotta go.' She squeezed Adam's hand.

'Remember what I told you.' She stood up to face Guy Chambers. Tall, with blond curly hair, big blue eyes, looking as if butter wouldn't melt in his mouth—and yet he was shaping up to be like the classmates who taunted Adam. A first-class bully.

And talk about bad timing. If he'd heard what she'd just said…would he think she'd been talking about him? Would that make him even worse? She glanced at the clock. 'Actually, our list starts in fifteen minutes so there's plenty of time to get ready,' she said coolly. 'Jenny knew where I was, or you could have paged me if something urgent came up.'

'I expect my staff to stay where I can find them,' he rapped out.

'Well, I know that now. It won't be a problem in the future.' Given his mood, she didn't quite dare ask for five minutes to fill Ben in on her findings. But there was one thing he couldn't deny her… 'I'll just go to the loo, if you don't mind.'

Three minutes. Enough to scribble Ben a quick note about Adam. And she'd have to be very, very careful in Theatre this afternoon.

'Have you seen much keyhole surgery, Fisher?' Chambers asked.

'Er—not really,' Paul said, flushing.

Kirsty noted that he didn't ask *her*. Obviously she was still in disgrace for daring to leave the surgical ward without his permission.

'We're presented with a case of chronic cholecystitis. Which means what, Fisher?'

'Inflammation of the gall bladder that's gone on for a long time.'

'Good. Symptoms?'

Paul seemed to relax, back on familiar ground. 'Vague digestive complaints—abdominal discomfort, flatulence, especially after rich or fatty foods, dull pain, nausea and vomiting.'

'Presence of calculi?'

'If there are gallstones, they'll grow larger in size or number as the condition goes on.'

Textbook answer, Kirsty thought approvingly.

'Jaundice?'

Paul thought about it. 'Not sure.'

Was he going to ask her? Kirsty waited. But, no, Chambers went straight into the answer. 'May be present if the inflammation involves the bile ducts. Other symptoms?'

'Scarring and thickening of the wall of the gall bladder,' Paul said.

'And cholestasis,' Chambers added. 'Well done, Fisher.' He gave Kirsty a look. 'And we'll remove the stones how, Brown?'

She'd have preferred him to have used her first name—or at least add her title to her surname, to be more courteous—but it was obviously his way and she'd have to lump it. 'If they're just in the gall bladder, either by cholecystostomy—drainage—or by cholecystectomy—removal. If the patient's already had the gall bladder removed but still has symptoms, we'd try ERCP,' she said. Endoscopic retrograde cholangiopancreatopgraphy, or ERCP, was where a combination of a fibre-optic endoscope and a contrast medium showed the location of gallstones, usually in the bile ducts. 'We'd need to measure the patient's blood coagulation levels, do cross-matching and check blood type, and give antibiotics and IV fluid before the procedure.'

He nodded. 'Major problems?'

'Haemorrhage and infection.'

'In this case, the gall bladder's still present so we'll do a cholecystectomy by laparoscope,' he said. 'Keyhole surgery means a faster recovery time.'

And Kirsty was itching to do this herself—keyhole surgery was what she really wanted to specialise in, something she loved even more than cardiothoracic work. Maybe she could learn from him. Maybe this would be the thing to smooth over the cracks in their working relationship.

He was thorough, she thought as she watched him remove the gall bladder and explore the bile duct for stones. He just needed to work on his people skills—not that she could suggest it. For a start, it wasn't protocol; and how could you tell a difficult person that they were hopeless with people, without making them defensive and their behaviour even worse?

She watched as he inserted a T-tube to drain the bile-duct.

'Close for me, Fisher.'

This time, he left Kirsty to supervise. Paul carefully closed, clamped the T-tube ready for transfer, and they accompanied the patient back down to Recovery.

'Are you OK with what happens next?' she asked Paul. 'Post-op care?'

'Attach drainage tube to receptacle, check tube for kinks, secure to dressing and lower bed linen and show patient how to turn over without pulling or compressing the tube,' he recited. 'Check dressings frequently for leakage or bleeding, check the patient is taking proper breaths instead of shallow ones, check nursing support for frequent coughing and breathing.'

She grinned. 'Spot on.'

When Mrs Morgan was settled, they walked down to the ward together. As they reached Chambers's office, she paused. 'See you later, Paul. I just want a quick word with Mr C.'

The back of her neck felt hot, but this had to be done. If she faced him now, they could clear up the problem quickly—if she left it, things could get even worse. She didn't want it to drag on and on and affect her work. She rapped on the door. 'Mr Chambers? Could I have a word, please?'

He looked up from his desk. 'Brown.'

She closed the door behind her and waited for him to ask her to sit down. He didn't, he just looked at her.

She took a deep breath. 'I think we need to clear up a problem.'

'Problem?'

Was he saying that it was all in her head? 'Mr Chambers, I get the impression that you don't like me very much. As we have to work on the same firm, I'd like to think we could overcome any personal differences on a professional level.'

'Really.'

The drawl made her want to slap his face. She wasn't the one in the wrong—she'd simply asked him not to touch her again, and she'd been perfectly calm and polite about it. She sighed inwardly. He wasn't going to give a millimetre, was he? 'I'm an experienced registrar. Why don't you make use of me?'

'What precisely are you offering, Brown?'

She flushed. She should have guessed he'd interpret it *that* way, given his groping habits. 'I'm used to operating. On simple cases, I supervise Paul and let him lead; on more complex ones, Tony used to let me lead and treated it as a teaching case for Paul.'

'And?'

'He used to ask us both questions.'

'Obviously he had confidence in you.'

She frowned. 'Of course. We'd worked together for a while. I was hoping you and I would be able to work together the same way.'

He leaned back in his chair. 'Tony gave you glowing references.'

What was she supposed to say to that? 'Yes,' was too smug, 'Did he?' was false modesty and 'No' was saying she had no confidence in herself and was useless at her job. She took refuge in silence.

He folded his arms. 'You were having an affair, weren't you?'

'What?' Kirsty stared at him, taken aback. 'Of course we weren't!'

He gave a little shrug, as if he didn't believe her. 'So you want to work with me the way you worked with Tony.'

'Yes.'

'Then I suggest you're as…accommodating with me.'

Surely he wasn't suggesting…? 'How do you mean?' she asked carefully.

'I think you know. Keep me happy…' to her disgust, he actually licked his lips '…and I'll see what I can do for your career.'

Meaning that if she didn't sleep with him, he'd make sure she lost her job? She didn't trust herself to answer. What she really wanted to do was to slap that nasty little smile from his face. In real life, that wasn't an option. Instead, she gave him one of her coldest glares and left his office.

He really thought she'd sleep with him to help her career? The sheer arrogance took her breath away. But what could she do now? If she went to Personnel, it was his word against hers. And a consultant's words were worth more than a registrar's. If she applied for another job, she'd have to ask someone else for a reference and the interviewer was bound to ask her why her immediate boss hadn't given her a reference. And if she stayed…

Then she remembered what Ben had said last night. 'Guy Chambers'll think you're unavailable so he'll leave you alone.'

Right now, that was the best option she had.

She paged him from Jenny's office.

Three minutes later, the phone rang. She snatched it up. 'Surgical.'

'Ben Robertson. You paged me?'

'It's Kirsty.'

'Kirst? What's up? Adam? I got your note. Well done for spotting what we'd all missed. He said you'd been dragged back to work.'

'No, it's not Adam, though I do want to talk to you about him later. It's what you asked me last night.' She swallowed. 'I've made my decision. It's yes.'

'Are you sure?'

No, but she was so angry with Guy Chambers that she suppressed her doubts. 'Yes,' she said tightly, and put the phone down before Ben could try to talk her out of it.

CHAPTER THREE

'WHAT made you change your mind?' Ben asked that evening, when they were sharing a Chinese takeaway.

'I thought about it, that's all. Your gran's important.'

'Hmm.' Ben didn't sound convinced but, to Kirsty's relief, he didn't push it. 'How was your afternoon with Dr Jekyll?'

'Haven't met him—just Mr Hyde,' she muttered with a grimace.

'Hey, it'll all come out in the wash. He's just the new boy trying to make an impression, that's all. Give him a couple of weeks and he'll be a pussycat.'

She didn't answer. If she told Ben what had really happened in Chambers's office that afternoon, he'd do his protective big brother act and warn Chambers off—and, in retaliation, Chambers would make her life hell. What had she said to Adam? That brains and technique won every time... Right now, she wasn't so sure that she believed it.

'So, are you on duty this weekend?'

'Yes, but I can swap shifts with someone if you want to go to Scotland.' She'd swap shifts with anyone—do double, treble even—if it meant not having to work with Chambers!

'Great.' He eyed the last pancake on the plate between them. 'D'you want any more of that crispy duck?'

'Yes, actually.'

'Spoilsport.' He expertly filled the pancake with hoisin sauce, duck and vegetables, wrapped it up, took a huge bite—then fed the other half of the pancake to her.

She was staggeringly aware of his nearness—of how

33

long and supple and strong his fingers were—and groaned inwardly. No. Don't say she was losing her immunity to Dr Charming. Not now. Not when the rest of her life was falling apart. This was one complication she could do without!

'You're going to have to work on that a bit,' Ben said, surprising her.

'What?'

'Me touching you. If you hadn't been sitting down just now you'd have leapt back six feet. My fiancée would be used to me being touchy-feely.'

She bit her lip. 'Sorry.'

'Hey.' He stroked her cheek with the backs of his fingers. 'It's me, remember? Ben. Best-friend Ben. I'm not going to do anything to hurt you. You know that.' He paused. 'What's your ring size?'

'I've no idea. Why?'

'For your engagement ring,' he reminded her. 'Gran'll expect it.'

'Tell her I can't wear a ring at work. It's not hygienic.'

'And you're a surgeon. I know, I know.' He smiled at her. 'Which is why you wear it on a chain round your neck at work.'

He was infuriating, the way he had an answer for everything. 'Ben, I—'

'By the way, I owe you one.'

She frowned. 'How do you mean?'

'My distraction case. Young Adam. How did you guess he was being bullied?'

She shrugged. 'He reminded me of someone I once knew.'

He gave her a searching look, but to her relief he didn't push it. 'He asked me to thank you. He said he was going to find out about martial arts.'

'Good.'

'I thought of alcohol abuse, maybe drugs—but I hadn't thought steroids,' Ben continued.

'Acne, aggressiveness and rampant testosterone,' Kirsty
recited dryly.

'Don't tell me. Takes a woman to see it?'

She chuckled. 'No. Actually, I was winging it. Lucky
guess.'

'If you're that good, you can pick my lottery numbers
for the next month.'

'If I was that good, I'd already have won it,' she
pointed out.

'Yeah. Well, I can dream. You go and sort your shifts
out—you'll need Friday afternoon off, too, because our
flight's at four—and I'll do the washing-up.'

'*You'll* do the washing-up?' she teased.

'I'm house-trained,' he protested.

'Barely.'

He grinned. 'And whose fault is that, Kirsty Brown?'

She pulled a face.

'Go and sort out your off-duty, woman, then run yourself a long bath and forget about Guy Chambers.'

If only, Kirsty thought, it was as easy as that.

She was on a late, the next day, whereas Ben was on an
early. Their breaks didn't coincide and, even if they had,
after the row she'd had with Chambers the previous day
she thought it politic to stay around the ward. She busied
herself talking to Elsie Morgan and a couple of other patients who were recovering from surgery, and kept her
nose firmly in her books when she was in the mess room.
Chambers ignored her on the ward and barely spoke to
her in Theatre; he only grudgingly allowed her to help
with retractors and suction.

Kirsty only just managed to rein in her temper. Why
was he treating her like a still-wet-behind-the-ears junior
when he knew she had the paper qualifications to back up
her position and her records showed she'd led several major operations, only calling Tony in when she'd needed
help? She hadn't slept her way up, whatever Chambers

claimed to think. She'd never even thought of Tony as a potential mate—he was twenty years older than she was, more like an uncle than anything else, and was going to celebrate his silver wedding to Helen next year.

But if Chambers thought it...did everyone else?

Damn the man. He'd managed to undermine her confidence and her trust in her colleagues in the space of five minutes.

Maybe, Kirsty thought, he had a point. If someone like *him* could put her off, maybe she wasn't cut out for the job. Maybe it was time to have a serious think about her future. She smiled wryly. At least she had someone to discuss it with. Ben would put her straight.

But he was out when she came home that evening. He hadn't left any scribbled notes for her beneath the salt-cellar—the place they'd agreed on years ago so they'd never miss an important message—so she stretched out on the sofa with an old film and a tub of ice cream. Wherever he'd gone, he wasn't back by the time she went to bed and he wasn't up by the time she left for work the next morning, though this time there was a message under the salt-cellar: 'See you at midday outside Jimmy's. I've booked a taxi to the airport. B. x.'

Late on the Friday afternoon, they were several thousand feet up in the air on a tiny plane from Southbay to Inverness. 'For you,' he said, handing her a beautifully wrapped parcel. 'It's a cheering-up present.'

A box that size couldn't contain a ring—so he'd obviously seen sense, she thought with relief. She undid the crimson ribbon, unwrapped the gold paper and beamed when she saw the embossing on the lid of the box. Her favourites. Hand-made white chocolates from the expensive confectioner's round the corner from Jimmy's. 'Oh, yes! Thanks, Ben,' she said, kissing him lightly on the cheek.

He coughed.

'What?'

'You're supposed to open them now.'

She narrowed her eyes. 'Why?'

'You know...' He made a rolling gesture with his hands. '*Share* them. They're my favourites as well, remember?'

'Typical. The man gives me a present and expects half,' she grumbled teasingly. She opened the box—and her eyes widened in surprise. Nestled among the chocolates was another box, much smaller.

A box that could only contain one thing.

'Open it,' Ben said softly.

She did, and she wasn't sure if the diamond nestled against the blue velvet was sparkling madly or if she had tears in her eyes. 'Ben...you didn't have to do this.'

'Gran'll expect it, remember?'

'Mmm.'

'Here.' Ben took the ring from the box, lifted her left hand and slid the ring onto her finger. A plain little platinum ring with a flat-cut diamond that did sparkle madly.

'It's beautiful.' She examined it closely. Amazing what they could do with silver and cubic zirconia nowadays. This looked exactly like the real thing—but, of course, it couldn't be. This was a fake engagement so it'd be a fake ring. Ben would be practical about it. 'And it fits,' she said in surprise.

'I borrowed the ring your parents got you for your twenty-first for sizing,' he admitted.

'And the box?' she asked, suddenly noticing that the silk lining the top of the box subtly bore the logo of the most exclusive jeweller in Southbay. A jeweller that definitely didn't sell cubic zirconias.

'It came with the ring, Kirst,' he said softly.

Her eyes widened. He *hadn't* been practical about it. In fact, he'd gone stark, staring mad! 'Ben, this must have cost you a fortune. I can't wear this! Why didn't you just get a cheap one?'

'Because Gran would know. And she'd ask why I hadn't bought my fiancée a proper ring.'

There was no answer to that. Kirsty took refuge in the chocolates.

When they landed at Inverness, they picked up the hire car Ben had booked and he drove them through narrow roads which had Kirsty alternately peeking through her hands at the incredible view of the loch and closing her fingers again so she couldn't see a car coming the other way.

'I thought surgeons were supposed to have nerves of steel?' he teased.

'We do, in an operating theatre. This is different. Ben, you're driving like a maniac!'

He chuckled. 'No, I'm not. There are plenty of passing spaces, and I know this road well enough not to take it for granted and start speeding. We're perfectly safe, Kirst.'

Half an hour later, she had to admit he was right when he parked outside his grandmother's cottage. Morag came out to welcome them, hugging both of them.

'It's good to see you again, Kirsty. Come in, come in,' she said. 'Ben, you bring the bags.'

'Yes, Gran.'

'And no cheek,' she warned teasingly. 'Kirsty, my dear, you'll have a cup of tea?'

'Please. I'll make it,' Kirsty said, following Morag into the large kitchen.

'No, no, lass. It's no trouble. Sit yourself down.' She waved towards the scrubbed pine table and chairs at the other end of the kitchen.

Kirsty eyed the table and the supper Morag had set out ready for them. Triangles of home-made bread draped with smoked salmon, light, fluffy scones with home-made raspberry jam, and oatcakes with a hunk of strong cheese and home-made tomato chutney. 'Wow.'

'It'll take Ben five minutes to finish that lot,' Morag said.

'Three. He's got help,' Kirsty corrected, and they both laughed.

Morag hugged her. 'I was so pleased when Ben told me. You're the right one for him. I knew it when I met you, all those years ago. And don't you go telling me you were just friends all along—I saw how you looked at each other, even back then.' She lifted Kirsty's hand. 'And what a beautiful ring. It suits you, lass.'

'Thank you.' Kirsty looked at her. 'And how are you, Morag? Really, I mean?'

'I'm fine. I've got my pills and I do what the doctor tells me.'

'As much as Ben does?'

Morag's lined face creased with laughter. 'I try. But I'm fine. It's really nothing.'

'Angina *isn't* nothing. It can be very frightening.'

'I'm old enough and wise enough to cope,' Morag reassured her. 'And you can tell Ben that, too.'

'Tell me what?' Ben asked, appearing in the kitchen with their bags.

'I'm perfectly all right, so I don't want any nagging from either of you.'

'I wouldn't dare, Gran.' He smiled at her. 'I'll take these upstairs, shall I?'

'Do. Of course, you've been together for so long,' Morag said, 'I'm not going to be old-fashioned about it.'

Kirsty's stomach lurched in warning. Old-fashioned about what?

'So I've put you in the same room,' Morag continued sweetly.

The same room? Morag was expecting her to share a room—a bed—with *Ben*? 'I—er...' Floundering, she looked at Ben.

Ben simply walked over to Kirsty and put his arm round her shoulder. 'Thanks, Gran.'

Wasn't this where he was supposed to make some comment about respecting his grandmother's generation and offer to sleep on the sofa?

But he didn't. Kirsty started to panic. She was wearing his ring—a very expensive ring, at that—and now she was sharing a room with him...

Somehow, she got through the rest of the evening, making light conversation with Morag. And then, at half past nine, Ben made things worse. Much worse.

'Gran, it's been a long day and Kirsty worked a half-day shift before we left. Would you mind if we had an early night?'

'Not at all. There's plenty of hot water and I've put towels in your room.'

Ben hugged his grandmother. 'Thanks, Gran. See you in the morning.' He hooked his arm round Kirsty's shoulder. 'Come on, you. Time for beddie-byes.'

Kirsty submitted patiently until they were in their room. Then she blew her top.

'I can't believe you just did that!' She kept her voice low, but the anger in her voice was clear.

'Kirst, she's made an effort to be modern. I couldn't throw it back in her face. It'd be rude.'

'I said I'd act as your fiancée, not that I'd *sleep* with you!' she hissed.

'Kirst, this isn't a long-drawn-out way of seducing you. Your honour's perfectly safe with me.'

Which made her feel even worse. She had to face it. Ben Robertson had the most gorgeous women at the hospital flinging themselves at him on a daily basis—so why would he even *look* twice at plain little Kirsty Brown, let alone anything else?

'You've had a long day and you're tired. Have a bath.' His lips twitched. 'I would offer to wash your back, but I think you'd take it the wrong way right now.'

'It's just...' No, she couldn't explain it to him. She couldn't explain what she felt to herself!

'Kirst, we've shared a room before. We had that all-night revision session when we were students, remember? You fell asleep on the end of my bed.'

Yes, she did remember. She'd woken up with her face stuck to her notes—and with Ben curled round her, his arm round her waist, pulling her back against his body, and his cheek against her back. It had thrown her a bit, but she'd decided it had just been tiredness and proximity. Ben hadn't meant anything by it. And she certainly wasn't going to wreck the best friendship she'd ever had by trying to make something of it and, three weeks later, being relegated to the ranks of Ben's ex-girlfriends. So she'd wriggled out from his arms and made them both a cup of very strong coffee and pretended nothing had happened.

'Go on. Bath. I'll be modestly attired by the time you get back.'

And he was. In tartan pyjamas.

Her lips twitched as she took in the sight. 'I don't believe you're wearing those.'

He grinned. 'I bought them specially for this weekend. What did you expect? Black silk boxer shorts?'

Her stomach gave a lurch. Ben in sexy undies... No, she didn't want to start thinking about that. They were just friends. Good friends. Very good friends...and this 'engagement' was purely to keep Morag happy and Chambers off her back.

'I thought we could go for a picnic by the loch tomorrow,' he said, clearly sensing her embarrassment and tactfully changing the subject. 'Gran said something to me about going out for a meal in the evening—there's a ceilidh in the village hall, tomorrow night.'

Ceilidh? Didn't that mean intricate dances? She panicked. 'Ben, you know I've got two left feet.'

'Even *you* can dance at a ceilidh, Kirst. It doesn't take long to learn the steps and your partner will always help you out if you get stuck. It's years since I've been to one, but they're great fun. You'll love it.' He patted the bed. 'Come on. Time to sleep.'

'Yeah.' She slid into bed beside him.

''Night, Kirst.' He kissed her lightly on the cheek and switched out the light.

Kirsty woke in the middle of the night, feeling warm and very comfortable. She was about to drift back into sleep when a few things suddenly hit her, and her eyes snapped open. Number one, the hem of her demure, baggy, knee-length nightshirt was somewhere above her waist. *Well* above her waist. Number two, there was a hand underneath said nightshirt—an arm encircling her waist and fingers curved round her naked breast. Number three, there was a male body curled spoon-style behind hers—an *aroused* male body.

She took a deep breath. Be sensible, Kirst, she told herself. You know it's a basic physiological reaction of the male in sleep—it's nothing to do with *you*. The fact he's touching you like that—well, that's just propinquity. You're his best mate, nothing more. He barely even registers you as female!

And if she tried wriggling out of his arms now, she'd wake him and they'd both be embarrassed and…it was easier just to stay where she was.

Except it wasn't. Was it her imagination, or had the neckline of her nightshirt slipped lower, too—and could she really feel his mouth against the curve of her neck, or was that just his breathing?

Her mouth went dry. This was crazy. She didn't think of Ben in those terms. So why was she suddenly imagining what it would be like if he touched her, gently rolled her onto her back and kissed his way down her body? Why was her nipple hardening under his touch? Why was she feeling that weird tingle deep inside her belly?

Because you're mad, Kirsty Brown, she told herself

crisply. It's not going to happen—and if it did, you'd lose him for ever. It's *not* worth it.

Sex wasn't anything to get worked up about. Hadn't she learned that the hard way, all those years ago, with Luke? Weeks of thinking that he loved her, that he wanted her…and all the time he'd had another motive in mind. A cruel, mocking motive.

Money. A bet. On how long it'd take him to seduce her.

Ben wasn't like that, she knew—but even so, nothing could ever happen between them. Even if Ben wasn't so gorgeous and she wasn't so plain, it still wouldn't work because he couldn't handle commitment. She wanted a man who'd stick by her—and Ben wasn't that man. Tonight…was an aberration.

She closed her eyes, told herself firmly to relax and stop being so silly. When that didn't work, she started counting sheep—except they were all wearing tartan pyjamas and reminded her too much of the male body curled round hers, with only the thin cotton of those same tartan pyjamas between them. Then she fell back on the old student standby of naming every single bone in the skeleton, followed by the major organs, the muscles, the arteries…and finally she drifted back to sleep.

Ben woke some time later, disoriented. He was in a strange bed and there was a very feminine form nestled snugly into his body. Her legs were entwined with his own—even her feet were—whatever she was wearing was pushed up well above her waist, so his hands were resting directly on her skin, and…

Oh, no. He suddenly remembered where he was. In his grandmother's cottage and sharing a bed with Kirsty!

He swallowed hard. There was no way he could move without waking her. And she'd be hideously embarrassed if she realised how entangled they were. He really ought to move his hand.

Bad idea, he thought as his thumb brushed her nipple and it hardened at his touch. Very bad idea. But he couldn't stop his thumb brushing her nipple for a second time and his fingers curving back round her swelling breast. It was a perfect fit. Beautiful, lush curves spilling out over his fingers...

This is Kirsty, remember? No sex, he reminded himself crossly. He didn't associate things like that with Kirsty. For goodness' sake, she was wearing the unsexiest nightie in the world, a big baggy thing with teddies on that came down to her knees.

Except right now it was nowhere near her knees. And he'd just discovered what sort of a body hid behind her white coat at work and the baggy T-shirts and sweaters or the huge, shapeless towelling robe she wore at home. A body he'd never actually seen in all the years he'd known her—they'd never gone swimming together and Kirsty wasn't one for sunbathing. A body that was much more delectable than he'd ever have guessed.

His mouth went dry. His body might be telling him to wake her gently, to touch her and kiss her and bring her to the point where they were desperate to be one, to let her body enfold his so he could take them both to paradise and back—but he couldn't. Get close like that and she'd change. He'd change. Their whole relationship would change—and he didn't want to lose her. Get involved, and they'd be ripped apart within weeks. Ben didn't do long-term relationships. Except friendship.

Kirsty didn't do relationships either. She was married to her career. Always had been. She'd been top of their class all the way through their student years, and he'd only done so well because she'd made him study with her. She was clever and bright and good with patients—he'd overheard her at work and she always managed to reassure anyone who was in a tizzy.

But she never went out, except in a group. If any man so much as approached her, he got a polite but very firm rebuff—she didn't even dance with anyone on the rare occasions he'd persuaded her to go clubbing. It was as if she had sworn off men for good. He was sure something had happened in their first year as students, but she'd always evaded the subject. And 'men', he thought grimly, would include him. He didn't want to lose the only other woman in his life who'd been constant.

This whole engagement thing had been one of his worst ideas ever.

It didn't help that Kirsty's hair smelt of apples and her skin smelt of the lemon shower gel she favoured. *Edible.* No. He wasn't going to start thinking about his mouth on Kirsty's skin. Or her mouth on his. Her hand stroking his back. Her legs twining round his waist and—

No. Oh, hell. If he moved now, she'd wake and she'd find out how aroused he was and the whole thing would disintegrate into a complete and utter mess. But if he didn't move, he wouldn't be able to stop his wayward thoughts. About seeing Kirsty's eyes all soft and almost golden with arousal, her body stretched out under his own, the softness of her skin sliding against his...

He swallowed hard and tried to keep his hand still. Except it seemed to have a life of its own and his fingertips were tracing her skin, teasing her nipple into full hardness and then slowly sliding down to her waist, lower, across the soft satiny skin of her inner thigh.

Stop it, he told himself fiercely. She's your *friend*. Plain little Kirsty. Though she wasn't plain, except in her own mind. She had a pretty, heart-shaped face and laughing brown eyes. Her soft brown hair had natural streaks of copper and bronze in it, and the body entwined round his right now was all curves...

She might be wearing his ring, but it wasn't a real engagement. He had no rights whatever where she was concerned. And he needed to remember that.

CHAPTER FOUR

THE next morning, when Kirsty woke, Ben was still wrapped round her—but not quite as much as he'd been in the middle of the night. Gently, she eased her way out of his arms without waking him, gathered her clothes and wash-bag and headed for the bathroom.

He was still asleep when she crept back into their room to deposit her nightclothes and wash-bag in her case. He'd moved so he was lying on his back, his left arm curved up above his head. He reminded her of a little boy, long sooty lashes against his fair skin and a half-smile on his lips. For a moment, she could imagine a little boy lying in that bed—her little boy, looking exactly like his father in sleep, though without the beginnings of stubble shadowing his face.

Then she shook herself. What on *earth* was she thinking? She wasn't going to get married and have children. Certainly not *Ben's* children. Cross with herself, she tiptoed out of the room and headed for the kitchen.

Morag was already there, tapping away at a laptop.

'Good morning, Kirsty,' she said with a smile, tapping a few more keys to save the file and switch off the laptop.

'Your web design stuff, I take it?' Kirsty asked.

'Indeed. Ben's bound to say I'm an old fool.' She grinned.

Kirsty shook her head. 'He's immensely proud of you, even though he probably doesn't say it. You're the most important person in his life.'

'No, love, that's you. Which is how it should be.'

She and Ben really had to tell Morag the truth. *Today,*

46

Kirsty decided. She couldn't go on deceiving Ben's grandmother like this. It wasn't fair.

But she wasn't going to do it without Ben being right there at her side. His lies, his mess—so he should fix it.

'Can I make you a cup of tea?' she asked.

'If you'll let me make you some porage. Proper Scots porage,' Morag emphasised.

'The way Ben makes it, with a tiny bit of salt?'

Morag chuckled. 'None of your brown sugar, honey or syrup in *this* country!'

'Not even heather honey?' Kirsty teased, then sobered. There was something she needed to know. And now, while Ben was asleep, was the perfect time. 'Morag... before Ben wakes. There was something I wanted to ask you.'

'Oh?' Morag turned enquiringly as she stirred a pot of porage.

'He worries about you.' Kirsty took a deep breath. 'He thinks you're not telling the truth about your angina—that there's something more seriously wrong.'

'My dear,' Morag began—and then they heard Ben's footsteps on the stairs. 'Later,' she said in an undertone.

Later. Kirsty took in the word, shaken. So Ben's instincts were right. There *was* something more seriously wrong—and Morag clearly didn't want her grandson to know. If all had been well, Morag would surely have said as much in front of him? But she wanted to talk to Kirsty later... Which meant that things were very far from fine.

Well, if Morag Robertson wanted to see her grandson happy and settled, that was exactly what she'd get, Kirsty determined. Whatever the problem was, however much time Morag had left, they'd make sure she was happy.

Ben walked into the kitchen, his hair still wet from the shower and his skin completely smooth again. Kirsty walked over to him, slipped her arms round his waist and dropped a light kiss on his mouth. 'I wondered if the smell of porage would wake you, Mr Sleepyhead.'

Ben's eyes widened. Kirsty had just kissed him! But…she'd been asleep when he'd woken in the night to find himself touching her. Surely he hadn't—she hadn't—they hadn't…?

Help!

Since when would a kiss from his best friend scramble his brain like this?

Since the middle of last night, a little voice in his head informed him. Since you woke up with her all warm and soft and very, very female in your arms. Since you discovered that sex is definitely a word you associate with Kirsty Brown.

She was looking expectantly at him, obviously waiting for an answer. 'Sorry.' He shook his head to clear it. 'What?'

'I said, you obviously aren't completely awake yet.' She rolled her eyes. 'Lucky there's one sensible person in this engagement.'

Then he realised. That kiss had been for Morag's benefit, not his. She was trying to tell him something in code. But what? He looked at his grandmother, and then his pretend fiancée. Was Kirsty trying to tell him she knew what was wrong with Morag? He had to get her alone—and fast! But how?

'Sit,' Kirsty directed, nodding to the table. She finished making tea for the three of them, and Morag ladled out two large bowls of porage.

'Yep, the same as Ben's,' Kirsty pronounced when she tasted it. 'Not that he cooks very often.'

'Oh, come on. I made you dinner the other night when you were late home.'

With an ulterior motive. He'd asked her to be his pretend fiancée. 'Makes a change from leaving crumbs behind you,' she shot back.

'Do you not normally eat together?' Morag asked, sounding surprised.

They stared at each other, aghast at how nearly they'd slipped up. Already.

'When we're on the same shift, we do,' Ben said lightly.

'If I'm not stuck in Theatre, dealing with one of his cases,' Kirsty added.

The potentially nasty moment averted, Kirsty turned the conversation back to something light. 'So where are we having this picnic, then?'

'On the shores of Loch Ness, of course,' Ben said immediately. 'Surely you want to see Nessie?'

'I've never seen her in my seventy-three years,' Morag said, 'and don't you tell any of your tall stories, Ben Robertson. You know what happens to liars.'

He flushed deeply. 'Um.'

'Your nose grows?' Kirsty guessed.

'You get spots on the tongue. Lots of them. The same colour as the lie,' Morag informed her.

At this rate, Ben thought, he and Kirsty both had extremely white and extremely spotty tongues.

They exchanged a guilty glance and ate the rest of their breakfast in silence.

Ben insisted on clearing up, to Kirsty's amusement—considering he always left his breakfast bowl in the sink so it needed a good hour's soaking that evening to get the hardened cereal off—and then on packing the picnic. It was weird to see him so domesticated. He looked… *married*.

Not that she should be thinking about marriage and Ben in the same sentence. If he ever settled down, it'd be with one of his tall, gorgeous women.

'So what time will the two of you be back?' Morag asked.

'Three of us,' Ben corrected. 'You're coming, too.'

'We came up to see *you*,' Kirsty added, 'not the scenery, beautiful as it is.'

Ben chuckled. 'You should have seen her last night,

Gran. You'd never have pegged her as a brilliant surgeon. She was a big feartie.'

'A what?' Kirsty asked.

'A feartie. You know, a scaredy-cat.' He winked and let his accent get even richer to emphasise the point that he was teasing her. 'Ye're a richt cooardy custard—even for a softie Sassenach.'

'Don't tease the lass, you bad boy,' Morag admonished him.

'I'll go and get my coat,' Kirsty muttered.

'Me, too,' Ben said, following her out of the room.

As soon as their bedroom door was closed, he looked her straight in the eye. 'Explain.'

'What?'

'The loving fiancée act. Gran's told you, hasn't she?'

Kirsty shook her head. 'She was about to, I think.'

He closed his eyes, shutting out the pain. 'I knew it. I *knew* she was hiding something.'

'Ben, I'm with you on this all the way. As far as she's concerned, you're happy and you're settled with me. That's the way we're going to play it, OK?'

'OK.' He swallowed, and opened his eyes again. 'It's just…she's all I've got, Kirst.'

'You've got me, too,' she reminded him. 'Best-friend Kirst, remember?'

'Yeah.' He struggled to smile. 'D'you think the ring's enough to convince Gran?'

Was he asking her to take it one step further and actually *marry* him? 'I don't know,' she mumbled.

'Maybe…' His voice was so soft that she looked up at him. He wasn't smiling. Those blue, blue eyes were intense. And they were focused on her mouth.

'Ben?'

Her heart skipped a beat as she remembered the previous night. Ben's body curled round her own. Ben's fingers touching her more intimately than any man since—

no, not since Luke. *Even* Luke. Luke hadn't bothered much with preliminaries.

And then Ben lowered his head. Hesitantly, as if he wasn't sure he was doing the right thing, as if he might be making a monumental mistake—until his lips touched hers. Gently. Softly. Even shyly, she thought with shock, as if he wasn't sure whether she'd push him away.

Which, of course, she ought to be doing. They were friends, not lovers.

But that didn't stop her hands coming up to tangle in his hair. Glorious, soft and thick hair. And once she'd done that it was as if she'd unleashed a dam—and she discovered why every other woman at Jimmy's dreamed of being kissed by Ben Robertson.

Because his kisses were incredible.

His mouth teased hers, nipping and caressing and cajoling until she opened her mouth, letting his tongue duel with hers. And his arms were round her now, pulling her hard against his body so she was left in no doubt about what the kiss was doing to him. His hand was stroking her bottom, kneading it gently, and the kiss went on and on and on, until the world seemed to be spinning round them.

And then he stopped.

'Thought we'd better have a practice run,' he said, though his voice sounded cracked. 'Just so we know.'

Colour flooded her cheeks. 'I beg your pardon?'

He had his back to her now so she couldn't see his face—couldn't tell what was going on in his head. 'We've never kissed. Properly, I mean. So I didn't want the first time to be in front of an audience.'

'What?'

'In case you pushed me away or slapped my face.'

There was still that strange, strained quality to his voice. Kirsty didn't understand. 'Why would I push you away?'

'Because you're my best friend and I'm not supposed to kiss you like that,' he informed her roughly.

Kirsty was suddenly back on Planet Earth. What had just happened between them hadn't been real. Not in his book, anyway. He'd done it so that if they had to kiss in public—as would probably be expected of a newly engaged couple—she would play her part and kiss him back for their audience's sake, not back off or slap his face or make a smart remark.

Suddenly, the sun coming through the window seemed a lot less bright.

She shook herself. Ridiculous. She'd agreed to do this, hadn't she? Especially after this morning, now Morag had as good as confirmed Ben's fears. She couldn't back out now—not without causing Morag a lot of needless hurt.

'Morag's waiting for us,' she said quietly. 'We'd better go back downstairs.'

Ben followed her down again, cursing himself. Kirsty looked as if she'd been thoroughly kissed, her lips reddened and slightly swollen. Hell, she *had* just been thoroughly kissed, and he still didn't understand why he'd done it. He just hadn't been able to help himself. Remembering how she'd felt in his arms, the softness of her skin against his, the way her body had responded to him even in sleep…

And now he'd just wrecked the best friendship he'd ever had. Because it would be the same as always—get too close and it'd all fall apart. So then she'd back off, probably end up moving out, and he'd lose her for ever.

You're a complete idiot, Ben Robertson, he told himself roughly. And it'd serve you right if she walked out on you right now.

Panic fluttered in his stomach. Kirsty wouldn't walk out on him—would she? Yesterday, he'd have said no, of course not. He'd have been confident. Today, now he'd kissed her…he wasn't so sure.

And he didn't like the feeling.

* * *

Morag didn't notice any tension between them—or, if she did, she didn't draw attention to it. She merely shepherded them out to Ben's hire car and insisted on sitting in the back, which left Kirsty's knees only a few centimetres from Ben's… Gulping, she slid her hand through the grab handle at the top of the window and held onto it for dear life. It wasn't just the narrow road that made her feel this nervous.

'Feartie,' Ben mouthed at her.

'Mad driver,' she mouthed back.

'Kirsty, you're perfectly safe with me. I've had two accidents, and neither of them were my fault—I was stationary at the time,' he said in a low voice.

'There's always a first,' she muttered. 'And these roads—'

'Are only dangerous if you take risks. Which I won't. You're perfectly safe with me.' He gave her a very quick sideways glance. 'And I'm nowhere near the speed limit, so you can stop braking.'

'I am *not* braking,' Kirsty muttered.

'Yes, you are. Typical surgeon—you don't like it when you're not in charge,' he teased. 'Gran, this ceilidh tonight—are we talking posh dress?'

'You won't need your "Prince Charlie", if that's what you mean,' Morag said.

'I didn't bring a dress or anything with me,' Kirsty said.

'Didn't bring a dress? She doesn't actually *own* one, Gran,' Ben added, laughing.

'A skirt's fine, lass.'

Kirsty didn't do skirts either. 'How about trousers?'

Morag chuckled. 'They're fine, too. Clothes really aren't that important. But you'll need pumps or ghillies—the floor can be a bit slippery. What size shoes do you take?'

'Five.'

'Perfect. You can borrow my spare pair,' Morag said.

'Thanks.' There was no way she was going to get out of dancing, Kirsty thought glumly. And Ben was probably good at it. He was good at everything.

Especially kissing.

No. She wasn't going to think about that.

'Kirsty?'

'Huh?' She hadn't realised he'd been talking to her. 'Sorry. I was…er…'

'Rapt in the scenery. I know. It's gorgeous. What I said was, I thought I'd drive us round the loch, then we'll have lunch at Drumnadrochit,' Ben repeated. 'That OK with you?'

'Fine.'

'Good.' As they drove round, Ben told her all about the history of the area, from ruined castles to cairns to the iron bridge. When Morag remarked how beautiful the walking was around Glenmoriston, Ben said immediately, 'I'll take you there next time we come.'

The way he was talking, Kirsty thought it was almost as if he really were her fiancé, making plans… But of course not. Forget that kiss. They were doing this for his gran, that was all—and she had to remember that.

'They pioneered trial marriages here,' Ben said, giving Kirsty a sideways look as they passed through one village.

'Trial marriages?'

'There's a special stone in the churchyard. The couple used to join hands in the hollow of the stone and agree to be married for a year. If they didn't have children in that time and their love cooled, they were free to go their separate ways.'

Separate ways. Just like she and Ben would have to go their separate ways. End their fake engagement, when he finally met the woman of his dreams…

Kirsty was silent until they finally reached Drumnadrochit.

'I know it's a bit of a touristy thing to do,' Ben said, 'but we just have to go Nessie-spotting.'

'Ben Robertson, remember your tongue,' Morag directed, laughing.

'Since you clearly want me to ask,' Kirsty said, 'have you seen Nessie yourself?'

'No.'

'And do you think Nessie exists, or are all those pictures fakes?'

Ben shrugged as he climbed out of the car and unlocked the boot. 'Who knows? Nessiteras rhombopteryx—that's our Nessie, to you—was first spotted in AD 565 by St Columba. Apparently, he drove the monster away by prayer.'

Kirsty took the picnic rug while Ben hauled the hamper. She linked her arm through Morag's and followed him down to a picnic spot at the side of the lake, where they spread the rug on the grass and sat down.

'A big-game hunter claimed to have seen it in the 1930s,' Ben continued, 'but he'd rigged the footprints with a stuffed hippo's foot he'd borrowed from the Royal Zoological Society.'

Kirsty laughed. She could almost imagine Ben plotting a prank like that as a child. 'But all the famous pictures—they were all fakes?'

He nodded. ''Fraid so. Expeditions with sonar equipment haven't found anything—but they haven't definitely disproved Nessie's existence either. And you do see strange things on the loch sometimes. I've been out fishing on it—there are weird currents across and below the surface, and people have seen sturgeon swimming across. Some people claim to have seen dolphins.'

'Surely it's too cold here for dolphins?' Kirsty asked.

He shrugged. 'Who knows?'

She stared across the deep waters. It was a cloudless day, warm even for springtime, and the lake was an unfathomable expanse of blue that reminded her of Ben's eyes. Ben's eyes, which were also becoming unfathomable these days.

'Ben, don't go filling the girl's head with nonsense. There isn't a monster,' Morag declared briskly. 'He's telling tall tales.'

And they'd both told Morag an even taller tale—that they were engaged.

She became aware that Ben was talking about the local wildlife. He sounded wistful—almost, Kirsty thought, as if he wanted to come home to settle down. And if he did that...would she ever see him again? His wife certainly wouldn't want Ben's plain little doctor friend popping up to see them, even infrequently. Especially if she had any idea that Kirsty was in love with her husband.

She closed her eyes momentarily. In love with Ben? Of course not.

And yet she couldn't get that kiss out of her mind. Or the way she'd woken up to find herself intimately tangled with him...

'Hmm?' she asked, aware that Ben was looking at her as if waiting for an answer.

'Scotland's really turned your head, hasn't it?' he teased. 'You're not listening to a single word I say.'

She flushed. 'Sorry.'

'All I asked was if you wanted a cup of coffee,' he said mildly.

'Oh. Yes, please.' Please, don't let her start being awkward with him.

Ben gave her a look she couldn't read, then unscrewed the lid from the flask, poured coffee into a mug and handed it to her.

'Thanks.'

Somehow she made it through the rest of lunch—chatting with Morag, teasing Ben and eating the glorious picnic he'd packed—and then Morag declared that she wanted to pop in to see a friend, and the young couple should have a romantic walk along the lochside.

They returned the rug and the remains of their picnic to the car, and then Ben slipped his arm around Kirsty's shoulders. 'Gran'll expect it,' he warned her softly, whispering in her ear to make it look as if he were making some lover-like private comment.

A little hesitantly, she slipped her arm around his waist, and they walked back down to the lochside. Though she noted that Ben didn't move his arm from her shoulder, even when Morag was well out of sight, and she felt too awkward to make a point of moving her arm from his waist.

They walked in silence for what seemed like hours. Kirsty didn't know what to say to break the tension without being inane. She couldn't stop thinking about the way he'd kissed her that morning. Worse still, she found herself actually wondering what it would be like if he kissed her again. Right now.

Then she felt his fingertips brush her jaw. She stopped and turned to face him.

'Kirst.'

Was he going to kiss her again? Her pulse quickened at the thought.

'Do you think Gran might…well, if I stay out of the way for a bit…tell you what's going on?'

'I'll do what I can,' she promised.

'Thanks.' He drew her towards him then—but his kiss was that of a best friend, on her forehead. Not a lover's kiss on her mouth. Not a kiss like he'd given her that morning.

Stop it, she warned herself. He might be Dr Charming but you're not Cinderella. You're not a tall, leggy blonde and you're most definitely not his type. He doesn't think of you in that way. This morning didn't mean anything to him, so don't make a big deal out of it.

She knew all that. She'd known it for years. So why did it hurt so much now?

CHAPTER FIVE

BEN in a kilt.

Kirsty hadn't been prepared for this. Not on the drive home, not when Morag had lent her a pair of dancing shoes and reassured her it didn't matter that Kirsty wasn't wearing a long skirt and a plaid fastened with a clan pin, not when she went to shower and change. She hadn't even realised Ben *owned* a kilt. He'd never worn one at a university or hospital do, to her knowledge.

And she certainly hadn't expected him to look so incredibly sexy in the kilt and plain white shirt. Sure, she and all her female friends had lusted after Mel Gibson in *Braveheart*, and, sure, she'd seen Ben wandering round their garden in a pair of cut-off denim shorts and nothing else on a really hot summer's day—but she'd had no idea just how gorgeous Ben would look in Scots national dress.

'It's the Robertson tartan,' he explained. A red background with narrow black lines and a mirror-image pattern of wider blue and green lines, some full and some in diagonal stripes, made the tartan look almost chequered. The red was a perfect foil to his dark good looks and the blue emphasised the colour of his eyes.

'I…um… It looks good.' She smiled ruefully. 'I should have guessed you'd have a kilt.'

'Only for formal stuff up here. Like I said, I haven't worn one for years.'

She had a piercing vision of Ben in the slightly more formal version of the outfit—with the addition of the short black jacket known as a 'Prince Charlie' making his eyes seem even bluer—standing at the altar in a tiny Scots

58

church, lit by candles, waiting for his bride to walk down the aisle towards him.

'Are you OK?' Ben asked.

Then she realised that she must have gasped at the stabbing pain she'd felt at the vision, knowing that the bride Ben was waiting for was someone else. Someone tall and slender with long legs, someone beautiful, a stunning vision in ivory silk and an antique veil. Not the woman who never wore skirts because they made her look even shorter and dumpier. 'I'm fine,' she lied. 'Just a bit nervous.'

'What about?'

'You know I've got two left feet. Remember our graduation ball?'

'I've still got the bruises,' he teased.

'That was just an ordinary dance—this sort of dancing involves the whole room! Ben, I'm going to embarrass you,' she warned.

'No, you're not.' He smiled at her. 'And the dances don't involve the whole room. Not all the time. Some of the dances are for couples—like the Gay Gordons—and some of them are for sets of couples, like Strip the Willow. And we won't be dancing all the time, anyway. Someone'll sing, someone'll play music and there'll probably be a round supper. Which usually means haggis, with a dram of whisky poured over the top.'

Haggis? Was this a wind-up—or was he really expecting her to eat sheep's intestines? Not to mention the fact she didn't drink spirits. 'I can't do it,' she said, panicking even more.

'Kirst, if you can perform open heart surgery, you can cope with a couple of dances at the village hall,' he reassured her. 'And I was joking about the haggis. There might be neeps and haggis there, but there'll be sandwiches and biscuits, too. And stop worrying about the dancing. I'll talk you through it if there isn't a caller.'

'Don't ceilidhs always have callers?' she asked, surprised. The weddings she'd been to had had a caller.

Weddings Ben had been to as well, she remembered, though he hadn't worn a kilt then.

'Down south, maybe, not usually north of the border. You grow up learning the dances at your parents' knees—grandparent's, in my case—so there's no need.'

'But what if—?'

'Someone else asks you to dance?' he guessed. 'That's fine. Just give them your soppy brown-eyed puppy look.'

'I do *not* have a soppy brown-eyed puppy look,' she said fiercely.

He chuckled. 'Yes, you do. You just don't use it very often. Kirst, everyone there will know exactly who you are. They know you're English and they'll assume you haven't done country dancing since infant school, except at the odd wedding. They'll help you with the steps. Just tell someone if you get stuck. They won't laugh at you or anything like that.' He tipped his head on one side. 'Don't make me say it.'

'What?'

'T.M.I.A.D.,' he said in a stage whisper. *Trust me, I'm a doctor.* Their private joke. Except right now it wasn't funny. She trusted Ben. But how could she go to this dance as his fiancée when she knew she was going to embarrass him—big time—in front of everyone from his home village?

Kirsty's nerves returned in full force when they walked into the village hall and changed their shoes. The ceilidh had already started and everyone was dancing reels, all without a single step out of place. The men were mostly dressed in kilts, except half a dozen whom she guessed to be English, probably newcomers to the village who had too much respect for the natives to wear a tartan they weren't entitled to. Likewise, most of the women were wearing the same sort of soft-soled lace-up dancing shoes she'd borrowed from Morag, teamed with long skirts and plaids. Even the women not wearing tartan—presumably the partners of the non-kilted dancers—were in long skirts.

Kirsty's trousers—despite being black, extremely well cut and smart—stood out a mile, and she wished herself a million miles away, to some place where she wasn't expected to dance and make a fool of herself!

Ben clearly sensed her nerves because he gave her a sideways glance and immediately put his arm round her shoulders. 'You look lovely. And stop worrying about the dancing, will you? You'll be an expert by the end of the evening. It's a great way to meet people,' he informed her.

People who'd be inspecting her and wondering why Ben Robertson had got engaged to a woman who was the complete opposite to his usual type.

She didn't get the chance to argue any more because one of the dancers stepped up to the microphone. 'Ladies and gentlemen, take your positions for the Gay Gordons.'

'Come on, Kirst,' Ben said, not giving her time to make an excuse, then talked her through the position for the dance. He slid his right arm over her shoulder, taking her fingers in his, and squeezed them encouragingly. But when he joined their left hands together, the butterflies in her stomach went mad.

Stop it, she told them silently. It's the way everyone's dancing. It doesn't mean a thing.

The butterflies had other ideas.

'Now four steps forwards. Count,' Ben whispered into her ear. 'The music has four beats to the bar so it's easy. Just count.'

His breath fanned against her skin, sending a shiver down her spine. She hoped he hadn't noticed it—or, at least, interpreted it as nerves about the dance. She was not, definitely *not*, going to start lusting after Ben Robertson. If she tried to have a relationship with Ben, she'd lose his friendship *and* have to find somewhere else to live.

Then she realised they were actually dancing. She didn't have time to be nervous, she was too busy counting steps and trying to remember what he'd said and letting his hands spin her round at the appropriate point. By the time the song was halfway through, she was starting to enjoy herself. And by the end she was won over. She could do this. With Ben beside her, she could do this.

She was prepared for a second dance—but not for what the woman at the microphone said.

'In case some of you hadn't noticed, our guests of honour have arrived.'

Guests of honour?

'We'd all like to welcome Dr Ben Robertson home,' she said. 'And his bride-to-be, Dr Kirsty Brown.'

Kirsty stared at Ben in horror.

He stared back, equally wide-eyed.

'You've kept it very quiet, the pair of you, but congratulations,' the woman continued, and the band played a few bars of the Wedding March.

'And there's a glass of champagne for everyone at the bar,' she informed them, 'to celebrate their engagement.' The band played another fanfare, and the woman reached out to pull a string. A banner unfurled to read HAPPY ENGAGEMENT, BEN AND KIRSTY, and there was a long round of applause punctuated by whistles and calls of, 'It's about time, too!'

'I don't believe this,' Kirsty muttered.

'It never occurred to me,' he muttered back. 'I never thought Gran would be so pleased she'd tell the world!'

'The buffet opens in twenty minutes. But now we're going to celebrate the happy couple's news with the St Bernard's Waltz.'

There were three or four other dances for couples—she ended up swapping partners for each of them, but it was fine. And everyone wanted to tell her how they'd really known for years that she and Ben would end up together.

'Ben's letters to Morag were always full of you. Kirsty

this, Kirsty that, right from the day he first met you.'
Robbie Forbes, the post office manager, smiled broadly
as he whirled her round. 'At least he chose a girl with a
Scots name!'

Ben's letters as a student had been about her? But what
about his string of girlfriends? The gorgeous blondes and
redheads with legs that went on for ever? Hadn't he written about *them*? Why her?

'Have you named the day yet?' Robbie continued.

'Er—no. When I've qualified. I still have to finish my
surgeon's exams,' she prevaricated.

'Don't leave it too long,' he advised kindly. 'When you
find the right one, you'll want the rest of your life together
to start right away.'

Except she wasn't the right one for Ben, was she?

'Of course, we all feel we already know you—even
though this is the first time we've actually met you,' Jim
Ramsay from the fish and chip shop said during the next
dance. 'And you're perfect for him. I know it's traditional
to marry in the bride's home town, but the parish church
up here's so pretty, it's a perfect spot for a wedding.'

'Er, we haven't really decided anything yet,' Kirsty
hedged, remembering her vision of Ben in a kilt down the
aisle of a tiny stone church, lit by candles, waiting for his
bride. 'There's plenty of time to sort out all the details.'

'I bet your parents are pleased you've a good man like
Ben.'

Her parents? She hadn't breathed a word of this to
them. Or to her brothers. Pleased? They'd lecture her for
days about being so stupid!

She was relieved when the caller told them to get in
line ready for the next dance, and Ben annexed her as his
partner.

'This one's the easier version,' he told her.

'Just spare me from the grillings,' she said feelingly.
'Everyone wants to know when and where the wedding's
going to be!'

'I'm sorry, Kirst.'

'Wasn't it your countryman who talked about tangled webs and practising to deceive?'

'I'll sort it out. I promise,' he said. 'But it looks as if Gran told the whole village. This is their way of welcoming you.'

If she'd been Ben's real fiancée, it would have touched her heart to know the village thought so much of him. As his fake fiancée, she simply felt as if she was lying to everyone. She *hated* lying. The fact they were all such nice, genuine, innocent people made it even worse.

The next dance passed in a whirl and by the time the band stopped, everyone was slightly red-faced and grinning.

'I need a drink!' she said to Ben, and they headed for the bar.

'Champagne for you both,' the barmaid said, handing them both a glass.

'Any chance of a long, soft drink instead, Sandy?' Ben asked.

'At your engagement? Don't be so daft!' came the retort.

With a rueful smile, Ben accepted the glass and handed one to Kirsty. 'Well—cheers,' he said.

'Will you not do the thing properly, Ben Robertson?' Sandy asked loudly. 'Give the girl a kiss!'

Ben retrieved Kirsty's glass. She could see mischief lurking in his eyes and she didn't trust that mild expression an inch.

He bent his head to her ear. 'If they want a show, let's give them one!'

And, before she could protest, he took her in his arms, arched her backwards as if they were doing the tango and kissed her. Very thoroughly.

By the time he lifted his head again, Kirsty was extremely flushed and feeling light-headed. And as she hadn't actually sipped her champagne yet, she couldn't blame it on that.

'This is meant to be a family occasion, not X-rated,' Sandy teased.

'You told me to do it properly,' Ben retorted, handing Kirsty her glass and draining his own. 'Kirst, my ain sweet one.' He was really hamming up his accent, she thought, too amused by it to be cross with him about that kiss. 'Will ye no' finish that so we can get back to the dance?'

She raised her glass in salute, drained the contents and set it back on the bar. 'Happy now, bonnie sir?'

'Bonnie's for girls,' he said in a stage whisper.

'What about Bonnie Prince Charlie?' she countered.

'Hmm. I'll concede that. But it's still mostly used to describe Scotland and pretty little girls with rosy cheeks, my bonnie wee Kirst.'

Kirsty glowered at him. She wasn't *that* little—and everyone knew she wasn't pretty. So why was he making such a big thing of it?

He merely smiled at her and steered her back to the main hall for more dancing.

The music and the atmosphere had got to her and she was really beginning to enjoy herself. If any of her brothers could see her now, she thought, they'd never believe their eyes!

She should have known that it was too perfect. In the middle of an energetic Strip the Willow there was a sudden crash. One of the dancers had tripped, she thought. And then the music stopped and it was clear that it was more than just a fall.

Ben and Kirsty went straight over to the fallen man. 'Marty McAllister,' Ben said as they drew near enough to recognise him. 'He's the local driving instructor. He got me through my test.'

'D'you need anything, Ben?' a woman asked as he knelt down beside Marty.

'Call an ambulance and get me some towels or something to put under his head,' Ben said, loosening Marty's collar. He had a nasty feeling he knew what it would be. Marty was in his fifties, smoked, was Jim Ramsay's best customer, was a good fifteen kilos overweight and had a job that pushed his blood pressure up—in short, he was a perfect high-risk candidate for a myocardial infarction, a heart attack.

'Marty,' he said gently, 'are you in any pain?'

'Just a bit of indigestion,' Marty said, wheezing slightly. 'Had it before but it's worse tonight.'

'Is it just in the middle of your chest?' Ben asked.

Marty shook his head. 'It's my left arm, too. Can't move it properly.'

Ben and Kirsty glanced at each other. Marty's face was still red and shiny from his exertions in the dance. Sweaty—healthy hot or worryingly cool? Kirsty put her hand on his forehead—it felt cold and clammy.

'Do you feel—?' Ben began, and his question was answered as Marty turned his head to one side and promptly vomited.

'Definitely an MI,' Ben said softly.

'How long will the ambulance take?' Kirsty asked in an undertone.

'Twenty minutes, at least,' Ben said.

Not soon enough.

'Your bag's at Morag's, isn't it?' she asked.

He nodded. 'I'll get it.'

'You stay here—he knows you. Get someone else to call the local GP for thrombolytic drugs a.s.a.p. I'll be back as soon as I can.' Kirsty went straight over to Morag and explained the situation. Morag gave her the house keys and Kirsty pulled off the soft-soled shoes and replaced them with her flat outdoor shoes before setting off at a run.

She'd seen this so many times before in patients where she'd done a bypass—fatty deposits or atheroma formed patchy plaques on the inner lining of the arteries, reducing blood flow and encouraging blood clots to form. The clots resulted in a sudden stoppage of the blood flow to the heart, so tissue in the heart muscle died, causing pain and making the heart pump blood less efficiently.

She knew Ben wouldn't have any thrombolytic drugs that would dissolve the blood clot but he'd have analgesics, so they could at least do something to ease the pain. And Ben'd have fluids in the bag, too, so they could put a line in if Marty went into shock. Hopefully the GP would arrive before the ambulance—the quicker Marty had drugs to dissolve the clot, the better his chances of surviving. As it was, his heart was likely to have an arrhythmia. Kirsty bit her lip. If his particular arrhythmia was the one known as ventricular fibrillation, which interfered with the heart's pumping action, he'd die without drugs or electrical defibrillation to bring his heart rhythm back to normal.

By the time she got back to the village hall, breathing heavily from her run, Ben had made Marty more comfortable. The bad news was that the GP was away on another call—they had to wait for the ambulance to arrive.

Kirsty took the analgesics from Ben's bag. He'd already called for a glass of water, so she gave a dose of the painkillers to Marty. 'These'll help the pain,' she said gently.

'What's going to happen to my Marty?' Ellen McAllister asked.

Ben looked at Kirsty and nodded slightly, signalling that he could cope with Marty on his own, and Kirsty drew Mrs McAllister to one side. 'He's had a heart attack, Mrs McAllister,' she said quietly.

'I told him! I *told* him! I told him those fags would kill him—that, and all the chocolate he scoffs. I've put him on diet after diet, and he sneaks out when my back's turned for some chips or a choc bar. His car's full of sweet papers. Oh, Marty!'

'I know. They drive you mad, men,' Kirsty said, trying to sound reassuring. 'Never listen to a word you tell them, do they?'

'That they don't,' Ellen said feelingly. She bit her lip. 'He'll be all right?'

'We'll know more when the ambulance gets here,' Kirsty said, 'because they've got a machine that can look at the way his heart's beating, and they'll have drugs to get rid of the blood clot that caused his heart attack.' Drugs she'd hoped they'd have got by now from the GP. Marty just *had* to hang on.

'Is he going to die?'

Difficult one. 'Nearly half of all people who have a heart attack live for more than a year afterwards,' Kirsty said carefully. Unfortunately, around forty to fifty per cent died within the first three weeks after the heart attack; she could only hope that wasn't going to be the case here. 'The ambulance will take him to the coronary care unit, where they can monitor his progress and treat any symptoms.'

'You're a heart doctor, aren't you? That's what Morag said.'

'I'm a general surgeon,' Kirsty said. 'But I do have a few heart patients, yes.'

'Will he have to have an operation?'

'Sometimes drugs will do the trick,' Kirsty said. 'They'll help his heart get back into the right rhythm and stop the heart being damaged further. Or they can put a little tube down his blood vessels to widen them—it's a procedure called angioplasty. What I do when I operate is called coronary artery bypass. That's where I take lengths of a vein from the leg and sew one end to the aorta—that's the main artery in the body—and the other end to a point below where the arteries are blocked. That's why it's called a bypass—the blood can be pumped through the heart as normal and bypass the blocked artery. While I repair the heart my patient's connected to a heart-lung machine. When I've finished, the patient comes off the machine and the blood flows normally again, then I wire the breastbone together and sew up the layers around the patient's heart, then his chest. Within a couple of days, he'll be back on his feet.'

'You make it all sound so easy,' Ellen said.

'It does take up to five hours,' Kirsty admitted, 'but it's the most common major heart procedure in the UK. Surgeons do around ten thousand a year.' She did a quick bit of mental arithmetic. 'That's around two hundred a week—so if that's what Marty needs he'll be in experienced hands.'

'He's had indigestion for days,' Ellen said grimly. 'Said he couldn't settle to anything.'

'They're all fairly common signs of a heart attack,' Kirsty told her. From the sound of it, Marty had already had a minor attack some time over the last few days. 'But you weren't to know, so don't go blaming yourself. These things happen. Sometimes people have a mild heart attack and they don't even have any signs. They're called silent infarcts.'

'And they really don't know they've had a heart attack?'

'Not until they have tests—which could be years afterwards.'

'I see.' Ellen turned back to Marty, her face lined with concern. 'I just want him to be all right. He was going to take early retirement next year. I don't think I could bear it if he, if he…' The sobs broke through her words.

'Help's on his way. He'll be in the best possible care within minutes,' Kirsty said, putting her arms round Ellen and letting her cry. 'And Ben's with him right now.'

'Your Ben. He's a good man.'

'I know.' Except he wasn't really *her* Ben. And, in the circumstances, there was no way she could explain that.

'I—I'm so sorry we've ruined your party.'

'It's not a problem.' Kirsty hugged the older woman. 'Marty's the most important one right now.'

At last they heard the siren as the ambulance arrived. Marty was swiftly moved onto a trolley and then into the ambulance. Ellen climbed in behind him and the now subdued crowd from the village hall gathered outside and watched the taillights as the ambulance drove away.

Ben's face was sombre. 'How was Ellen?'

'She wanted to know if Marty would be all right.' Kirsty sighed. 'Just pray he doesn't go into VF on the way.'

'Yeah.' Ben bit his lip. 'Why does it always have to happen to the nice ones?'

'I know.' She sighed. 'The stats I read last week say MI figures are down so the healthy living message is getting through at last—but when it happens to someone you know it doesn't feel like it, does it?'

'Ah, Kirst.' He slid his arm round her. 'I wish—'.

But she never did get to hear what he wished. Morag came over to them. 'Are you two all right?'

Ben nodded. 'But I think I ought to go to the hospital and find out how he is.' He reached over to hug his grandmother. 'Gran—thanks for the party. You've made it really special for us. And I wasn't expecting anything at all like this.'

'If I can't make a fuss of my only grandchild and the girl he loves,' Morag said, 'then it's a poor old world. I'm just sorry the party turned out like this.'

'None of us were to know. And at least it was here where we could help him, rather than if he'd been behind the wheel of his car,' Ben pointed out. He sighed. 'Go back inside and enjoy the rest of the party. I'll be back as soon as I can.'

'I think the party's dispersing anyway,' Kirsty said softly. 'I'll come with you—unless you'd rather I stayed with you, Morag?'

'Go with Ben.' He needs you, Morag's eyes added.

CHAPTER SIX

BEN drove them to the hospital. Although it was still rel-
atively early on a Saturday night, most visitors had obviously gone home because it was easy to find a space in
the hospital car park. They had enough change between
them to feed the parking meter, and at last they were
striding down the corridors to the coronary care unit.

At first, the receptionist didn't want to give them any
information because they weren't family members.

'I understand your position,' Ben said quietly, 'but
we're here in a professional capacity. We're both qualified
doctors—we were there when Marty collapsed and we
followed the ambulance in. I'm Ben Robertson, A and E
registrar at St James's in Southbay, and this is Kirsty
Brown, surgical registrar at the same hospital.'

'Ah.' The receptionist sighed. 'Then I'm sorry to tell
you, Mr McAllister passed away in the ambulance.'

'Marty's dead?' Ben blinked in disbelief. 'No. No, he
can't be.' He squeezed his eyes tightly shut. 'I should
have been able to do more for him.'

'I'm sorry,' the receptionist said again.

Ben opened his eyes again. 'Is Ellen still here? His
wife?'

A doctor who was passing stopped dead. 'Ellen
McAllister, is that?'

'Yes.' Ben forced a smile to his face. 'I'm—'

'Ben Robertson.' The doctor smiled back at him and
pushed her near-black fringe from her eyes. 'I thought I
recognised you.' She lifted an eyebrow. 'Forgotten me
that quickly, eh? Shona Livingstone.'

'Shona? Wee Shona? I didn't know you'd become a medic.'

'Hoping to be SHO in the next shift-round.' Her blue eyes appraised him swiftly and approvingly. 'I didn't know you were home.'

'Just for the weekend. I...' He seemed suddenly to remember his manners. 'Kirst, this is Shona Livingstone, an old schoolfriend. Well, she was three years below me, but we were, well, friends.'

He was blushing. He was actually *blushing*, Kirsty thought, shocked by the sudden stab of jealousy. Shona Livingstone had obviously meant a lot to him at some point. Had she been his first girlfriend or something?

'Shona, this is Kirsty Brown.'

'A friend from work?' Shona asked.

Kirsty couldn't stop herself saying it. 'His fiancée, actually. We've just followed the ambulance in.'

'Oh.'

Was it her imagination, or was there a sudden coolness in the young doctor's manner towards her? And if Ben asked her why she'd said it, what on earth was she going to say? She shook herself. It was obvious. Shona knew Morag, so she had to believe in the fake engagement, too—the last thing they wanted was for someone else to tell Morag the truth.

'I'm sorry to tell you both, he went into VF in the ambulance.' It was what Kirsty had worried about. 'They tried defibrillating him but...' Shona shrugged.

The first few hours after a heart attack were critical. Kirsty and Ben both knew that. But it was still hard to register—the man who'd danced with them at the ceilidh to celebrate their engagement was dead.

'Is Ellen still here?' Kirsty asked.

Shona nodded. 'In the relatives' room, if you'd like to see her.' She led them through to the room where Ellen was sitting next to a nurse, a cup of something hot and sweet in front of her, looking blank and disbelieving.

'Oh, Ben. My Marty… I told your Kirsty, he was retiring next year, and now…'

'I'm so sorry, Ellen,' Ben said, hugging her. 'If only I'd done something more.'

'You couldn't have done any more, lad. They've already told me that. They said even if Dr Cassidy hadn't been out on call and had given him the drugs you asked for, Marty still might have had another attack in the ambulance.'

'We're so, so sorry,' Kirsty said, sitting next to Ellen and putting her arm round the older woman. 'If there's anything we can do—anyone we can ring for you?'

'Our Andy's away at college in Newcastle—he'll be out on a Saturday night so there's no point trying to ring him now.' Ellen shook her head. 'And Marty's mother doesn't even remember his name most of the time. She's been in a nursing home for years. Alzheimer's,' she explained. 'I can't face telling her tonight. No, it's just me.'

'We'll take you home. Stay with you tonight, if you like,' Ben offered.

'No—I want to stay here a while yet. Anyway, it's your party in the village. You can't miss that.'

'We're not leaving you. We'll stay until you're ready,' Ben told her. 'We'll wait for you in the cafeteria. Take as long as you need.'

Ellen's face crumpled. 'What am I going to do without him? He was my best friend.'

My best friend. Just as Ben was Kirsty's. And what would Kirsty do without Ben? Her arm tightened round Ellen as she thought about it. Yes, she'd be just as bereft.

They spent a couple of hours in the cafeteria waiting for Ellen. Ben rang Morag and left a message on the answering machine to let her know what was happening. He also rang Ellen's neighbour, Linda Barrett, to make sure someone would be there when they brought her home. He and Kirsty sipped their overbrewed coffee while they waited.

'Ben.'

'Mmm?'

'I'm sorry. You clearly thought a lot of him.'

Ben nodded. 'I went through a bit of a wild stage in my teens. Marty straightened me out. He taught me to drive.' He smiled wryly. 'Before I was seventeen. On private land, so we weren't breaking any laws. He taught me to fish, too.' He sighed. 'And even then he ate all the wrong things in the wrong quantities. The picnics he used to pack…they were a dietician's nightmare. I should have made more time, Kirst. Come home more often. Talked to him.' Which proved he was like Sarah. Never made the time, never came home, never talked. Not when it was important.

'Ben, don't blame yourself. His GP probably nagged him until he was blue in the face. Ellen herself said he sneaked out to get chocolate and chips if she put him on a diet. He wouldn't have listened to you.'

'He might have done,' Ben said stubbornly.

'It wasn't your fault. You heard what Shona said. You couldn't have stopped him going into VF.'

He clenched his fists until the knuckles showed white. 'All the same, I should have been able to do something. I'm an A and E doctor, Kirst. I'm supposed to save people's lives.'

She took his hand, rubbing his fingers until he unclenched his fist. 'Ben, you *do* save people's lives. But you know as well as I do that you can't save everyone. It wasn't your fault.'

'I should have been able to help.'

Distraction needed, she thought. 'Tell me about Shona.'

He stared at her in surprise. 'Shona?'

'Shona. She obviously expected you to remember her.'

'Yeah. She was three years below me at school. She, um, had a bit of a crush on me. Though I just thought of her as my schoolmate's baby sister.' He rubbed his jaw.

'One Valentine's Day, the postman delivered the biggest card in the universe to Gran's house. For me. Everyone in the village knew it was from her. It took me *years* to live it down.'

'So that's why you were blushing when you saw her again?'

'I was *blushing*?'

'Mmm-hmm.'

'Well. She's the only girl ever to have embarrassed me to that extent.' He rolled his eyes. 'You know how it is when you're fourteen.'

'You were fourteen?'

'She was eleven,' he confirmed.

'And now you're both grown up. Both doctors.' Perfectly suited to each other. Shona was exactly Ben's physical type—tall, slender, long legs, long hair—and her blatant appraisal of him had made it obvious she'd be happy to take up where they'd left off.

'And I live on the other side of the country,' Ben pointed out, as if he'd read her mind.

Plus, he had a fiancée. Though neither of them wanted to voice *that* fact.

Finally Ellen arrived, breathless and apologetic. They made her sit down to drink a cup of hot sweet tea, then drove her home. The neighbour Ben had phoned earlier was there waiting for them, so Kirsty and Ben returned to Morag's house.

Morag had already gone to bed and had left them a brief note telling them they didn't have to get up early in the morning.

'I don't know if I'm going to get much sleep,' Ben said.

'You're not staying up all night, brooding. It won't solve anything and it won't bring Marty back,' Kirsty told him firmly. 'Bed. I get the bathroom first.'

This time she was the one modestly attired when he came to bed, still slightly damp from his shower.

'Goodnight,' she said quietly, and switched her light off.

Silence stretched out between them as they lay there, side by side, not touching, completely rigid. Both of them could remember the previous night—waking up to find themselves entwined.

And neither of them dared to broach the subject.

'Kirst?' Ben said finally in the darkness.

'Mmm?'

'I could do with a hug.'

A hug. That meant just lying in each other's arms. She could cope with that—couldn't she? They'd hugged plenty of times in the past. A hug. 'Me, too,' she said softly. She really, really could do with a hug.

And then they really were lying in each other's arms. Holding each other. She could feel every beat of Ben's heart—and she'd have bet good money that he could *hear* every beat of hers.

He moved slightly, and his cheek was against hers. Cheek to cheek. Just as if they were dancing together.

He moved again, and his lips touched her cheek. Soft. Tentative. Questing.

Her heartbeat got louder.

Another feathery kiss on her cheek.

Her heartbeat got louder still.

This time, just before he kissed her cheek again, she moved. His lips met hers. Very softly, very gently. He nuzzled his nose against hers. Kissed her again. And again. This time, she opened her mouth and touched the tip of her tongue to his lip.

That was when his kiss turned wild. Ravishing. Desperate, as if she were the only thing stopping him from being sucked under.

She wasn't sure quite how he'd managed to remove her nightshirt—or how she'd managed to remove his pyjamas—but finally they were skin to skin. His hard body was pressing against hers. The hair-roughened texture of his skin grazed her nipples and she moved against him, her breasts starting to swell with desire. The butterflies in her stomach were going really crazy now.

'Sweet, beautiful Kirsty... My Kirsty, my love...' The words were so soft, she wasn't sure she'd heard them. But she wasn't in a position to think. Not when he was trailing kisses down the side of her neck like that. Gentle kisses—and yet demanding at the same time, demanding that she open her body to him.

She arched back against the soft feather pillows, lifting herself slightly, and Ben's mouth slipped lower. Lower. Until finally he took one nipple into his mouth and sucked.

She shuddered with pleasure, and he transferred his attention to the other breast, moving from one to the other until her hips started bucking.

Then he moved lower.

No. Surely he wasn't going to...? But as his lips grazed the soft inner skin of her thighs, she realised that was exactly what he was going to do. Something Luke had never done. He'd never been particularly concerned about her pleasure. She stiffened, nervous and unsure. Ben stopped what he was doing, sensitive to her mood, and moved to lie beside her.

'Kirsty. Sweet Kirst. Don't be scared. Not of me. I'm not going to hurt you.'

Oh, but, yes, you are, she thought. Because you don't do commitment—and I don't want to be your best friend any more. 'I want... I want...'

His voice was deeper now, amused and aroused. 'You want what?'

She went scarlet. Heavens, how much had she said aloud?

'Kirsty. You just said, "I want,"' he reminded her.

'Mmm.'

He chuckled, a low, deep sound. 'And you're not going to tell me? Well, I know what *I* want, Kirst. I want you to touch me. I want to touch you. I want to taste you.' His voice became even huskier as he added, 'All over.'

'Ben, I…'

He moved so he was no longer touching her. 'Oh, hell, Kirst. I'm sorry. I hardly know what I'm saying.'

She didn't have to be told. If he could turn down someone as beautiful and glamorous as Shona Livingstone, he'd have to be in a real state to pick plain little Kirsty Brown as his lover.

'It's just—just delayed shock. About Marty, I mean,' she said, trying her best to sound sensible.

'I know. I'm sorry. I should—'

The words were out before she could stop them. And they most definitely weren't sensible. 'Celebrate life.'

There was a long pause. A very, very long pause.

'What?' he croaked.

'Celebrate life. We should, I mean.' Her voice wobbled slightly.

He moved closer. 'Kirst, are you telling me…?'

'That we've had a hell of an evening, we both need comfort, and…who else do you turn to but your best friend?'

But I don't have sex with my best friend, he thought savagely. I don't go up in flames when she kisses me. I don't… Hell. He didn't want to lose Kirsty. She'd been part of his life for so long—he'd be lost without her. As lost as Ellen McAllister without Marty, her best friend. And her husband.

Husband.

Ben didn't do commitment. They both knew that. The ring on Kirsty's finger was purely to keep his grandmother happy—his gran, who could even now be in the same situation as Marty McAllister. This wasn't fair to either of them. He had to stop now, before he hurt her.

'Kirsty, it's kind of you,' he managed to say finally, backing off again, 'but I'm not going to use you like that. I'll sleep on the floor.'

*   *   *

In other words, I'd rather wake up with a dodgy back and a crick in my neck than make love with you, Kirsty thought. Well, she had her pride. She wasn't going to beg him. 'Don't be silly. We shared a bed last night, didn't we? There's no difference tonight.' Except I tried to seduce you in a moment's madness, and you turned me down. And as for you calling me your love—I probably just heard what I wanted you to say. 'Stay where you are.'

'You're right. Sensible Kirst. You're always right,' he said.

Though she noticed that he didn't make a move to put the tartan pyjamas back on. And she didn't dare put the light on to try to find her teddy-covered nightshirt. They lay there, side by side, not touching, both pretending to breathe regularly and deeply. Sleep was a long time coming, but at last it arrived for both of them.

Kirsty woke in the middle of the night. She was warm and comfortable and… Ben was wrapped round her again. Except this time neither of them was wearing a stitch of clothing. She could feel every hair on his chest against her back. And on the hard thigh nudged firmly between her own.

She swallowed hard. His thumb was circling her nipple. He was touching her in his sleep. Stroking the dusky pink tip of her breast until it hardened. And his mouth was definitely against her shoulder. She could feel his lips against the sensitive spot at the curve of her neck, kissing her. Very lightly, very softly, but definitely kissing her.

Unable to help herself, she wriggled her bottom against him.

The hand playing with her breast stilled instantly.

If he moved away now…

But he didn't. Unbelievably, he didn't. His hand was stroking across her abdomen. Sliding lower. And then he was touching her intimately. She could hardly breathe as his fingers skated against her skin and he explored her until she was quivering with anticipation and need.

Without a word, she turned to face him. He rubbed his nose against hers, then kissed her. Gently at first, then more deeply, until she felt as if a fire was raging through her. She wanted him. Wanted him so badly. Wanted him to touch her and taste her and *take* her.

He moved them both so she was lying on her back again and he was on top of her, and slowly he moved down her body, touching and tasting and arousing her until she was almost howling with need.

A need that Ben shared. When he spoke, his voice was ragged. 'Kirsty. I need you.'

'Now,' she said, her voice as husky as his.

There was a moment's pause and some rustling as he moved to protect her, and then finally he entered her. Kirsty moaned softly against his shoulder and he waited, letting her body adjust to his before he thrust deeper. She wrapped her legs round his waist, and he lost it completely. Kirsty was everywhere. Touch, scent, taste, sound…all Kirsty. The only sense missing was sight, and he knew if he put the light on, as he craved, to watch the expression in her eyes as he drew them both on to climax, they'd both realise what they were doing and pull apart again.

Right now, it didn't matter that it was crazy. It didn't matter that they were risking everything. It didn't matter that he didn't do commitment and she didn't do relationships and this whole engagement thing was to take the pressure off both of them in different ways—all that mattered was the way she felt beneath him, soft and warm and giving and incredibly passionate. All that mattered was the way she murmured his name, the way her body slowly began to ripple round him, the way his body surged in response…

So this, Kirsty thought, was what all the fuss was about. She'd had no idea.

CHAPTER SEVEN

ACCORDING to the clock on the bedside table, it was nearly ten o'clock. She ought to get up. But Kirsty felt lazy and drowsy and, with Ben's arms wrapped firmly round her, warm and comfortable.

Ben.

Her cheeks heated. Facing him was going to be…difficult. After the way she'd thrown herself at him last night, she wasn't sure if she could ever face him again!

And, besides, now she knew. Now she knew why women swooned over Ben and why women made such a fuss about sex. What had happened with Luke all those years ago was so far removed from what she'd experienced last night… She could only describe it as lust. *Uncontrollable* lust. Because she and Ben hadn't stopped at making love just once. They'd reached for each other again and again, gorging on each other's bodies. Exploring each other—touching, tasting, doing all sorts of things she'd never done before which had left her faintly stunned at the idea until Ben had introduced her to the sheer pleasure of the reality.

It was all down to experience. She knew that. Ben had had—well, she'd lost count of how many girlfriends he'd had. And most of them had been his lover as well as his girlfriend. They must have been. Whereas she… There had only been Luke.

What a lot she'd missed. A whole world.

And Ben had been the one to complete her education.

She screwed her eyes tightly shut. She didn't want to lose Ben's friendship. Yet his girlfriends only ever lasted a matter of weeks—he wasn't into commitment and he made it clear right from the start so no one got hurt.

This time, it was different. Neither of them had intended this to happen—but it had. And she had no idea how they were going to work it out.

What the *hell* had he done?

He'd just managed to wreck the best friendship he'd ever had. How could he have been so stupid? Yes, he'd been upset about Marty's death, and he was worried about Morag, and Kirsty had been there—but he really, really shouldn't have done it. Sex plus best friend equalled very, very bad idea. How was he ever going to salvage this mess?

He couldn't blame Kirsty. It hadn't been her fault. She'd just responded to him. He shouldn't have been touching her in the first place. She was completely off limits. What he'd done had just changed everything. And now, on top of everything else, he'd probably have to find somewhere else to live. How could they possibly share a house as friends after this?

Stupid, stupid, *stupid*, he raged silently.

Worst of all, he knew he would hurt her. It was the only possible outcome. He'd always been so careful to make sure his partner knew the score, that it would be fun, pleasure for them both, but definitely not a ticket to happy-ever-after land. He didn't want commitment. He really, really didn't want marriage and two point four kids and a dog and a cottage with roses round the door and hollyhocks in the front garden. And Kirsty... He'd asked her once why she never dated. She'd said she wanted to concentrate on her career. But she was heading for thirty—the time when many women's biological clocks started to tick. Had *he* started her clock ticking by giving her a proper engagement ring and making love with her? If he had, after what they'd shared last night, would he be the one she wanted to settle down with?

He couldn't be so selfish as to expect her just to have sex with him and still be his best friend when it fizzled out. Because it *would* fizzle out—it always did. Yet now he'd made love with her…he didn't think he could live with her platonically either. Last night had been incredible. He hadn't been able to get enough of her. Even now, he wanted her. He wanted to touch her, taste her; he wanted her to touch him, too, stroke his skin and kiss him and—

He didn't do relationships.

But it didn't stop him wanting to kiss the nape of her neck, nuzzle her shoulder, turn her round in his arms and lose himself in her.

What a mess. What a complete and utter mess.

He knew Kirsty was awake. Although she hadn't said a word and her breathing was still deep and regular, she was unnaturally still. Which meant she was trying to make him think she was asleep until… What?

Face it, he thought. They both had to face it. The sooner, the better. He stroked her hair. 'Kirst? You awake?'

She shifted so that she was facing him. 'Ben.'

There was a very, very long pause.

'About last night…' they both began.

They both stopped and smiled.

'Great minds think alike,' he quipped.

'Last night. We know what it was. Just comfort—celebrating life,' said Kirsty.

It happened with most medics at some point, Ben thought. It was their way of coping with losing a patient—their way of facing the future and reminding themselves that life had to go on. They'd lost Marty, and then they'd…acted out of character.

'It doesn't change anything between us,' Ben said.

'Of course not. We feel the same way,' Kirsty echoed.

'Yes.'

'We're still friends.'

'Still friends,' he confirmed, relieved. And yet part of him was…what? Disappointed? Crazy. He didn't want commitment. Why should he be disappointed that she didn't either?

'That's good.' She dropped a kiss on the end of his nose. 'I need a shower.'

'Go ahead.'

She coughed. 'Um, do you mind closing your eyes?'

Closing his eyes? After what they'd done together last night, she was *shy*? He smiled indulgently. 'Of course.'

'Thanks.' She retrieved her nightshirt and pulled it on. 'See you in a bit,' she said, giving him his cue to open his eyes again.

She was covered to well below the knee, those beautiful curves hidden behind the baggy cotton. Probably just as well, he thought wryly. If he had a visual reminder of what she'd felt like in his arms, he'd probably pull her back into his bed and to hell with the consequences. Consequences that would catch up with them in the end. No, this way was better. The sensible way.

'See you in a bit,' he echoed.

He stayed in bed, thinking, after she closed the door. Kirsty had made it very clear that last night had been a one-off. 'Comfort—celebrating life,' she'd said. Meaning that it had been just sex for her.

Sex. Not the best thing to think about, he acknowledged wryly as his body informed him that sex with Kirsty was just fine and dandy, as far as it was concerned. You just didn't have sex with your best friend—particularly when she was heading for the top in her chosen career and wouldn't allow anything else in her life to get in the way.

And he ignored the very soft voice in his head that asked if it had really been just sex for him, too. No way was he going to start considering that.

Kirsty turned the shower onto its coldest setting. Even the jolt of the icy water didn't seem to work. Instead of feeling relieved that she wasn't losing him, she felt…bereft.

But what else could she have done? Clung to Ben and told him she loved him? She knew he wouldn't have pushed her away—he had too much innate kindness to reject her like that. He'd have been gentle with her, then gradually distanced himself again. Because he didn't do commitment, all the women in his life were temporary. She was only a permanent fixture in his life because she was his best mate—he didn't even think of her as female.

Except he had last night.

And he'd shown her just how very female she was.

She turned the shower back to warm and scrubbed her skin harder. No. She wasn't—absolutely wasn't—going to think about sex and Ben at the same time.

Or love.

She stopped scrubbing. Love? She'd thought herself in love with Luke. Now she knew it hadn't even been infatuation—it had been very pathetic gratitude at an attractive male actually asking her dumpy eighteen-year-old self out. The kick in the teeth had come later, when she'd found out why Luke had really asked her out, and that it had had nothing to do with her attractiveness—more like her lack of it.

But this… How did she feel about Ben? Half the time, they didn't have to say anything because they knew exactly how each other thought. But that was from years and years of knowing each other, talking and sharing their lives. Friendship, that was all. Except now she had to add lust. And friendship plus lust was a completely different equation.

Love.

She loved Ben?

But he didn't love her. At least, not in that way. Because she knew her algebra: if friendship plus lust equalled love, love minus lust equalled friendship. And

Ben didn't lust after her. Last night had just been comfort, that was all.

Could he ever grow to love her? Right now, she couldn't answer that. She knew how she felt about him—but how could it ever work out? Ben didn't trust anyone enough for commitment. Someone had hurt him very badly in the past—it was something they'd never discussed but she instinctively knew that. It had to be why he was too scared to trust. But would he let her teach him how to trust?

No. Of course not. He saw her as a friend, and after what she'd told him this morning he thought she felt the same way. So best friends it'd have to be. Until he was ready for something more—if ever.

By the time Kirsty returned to their room, dressed but with a towel wrapped turban-style round her wet hair, Ben was up, clad in faded jeans and an old rugby shirt, and was in the middle of packing. 'Gran's at church, but she's left a casserole in the oven.'

Kirsty frowned. 'We should have gone, too.'

'No one expects it, Kirst. We were at the hospital until late last night, remember?'

And then… Her face heated. No wonder they'd slept in so late this morning. 'Yes.' Embarrassed, she turned to her packing.

'I'll go and make us some coffee,' Ben said.

'Thanks.'

She finished packing, combed her damp hair, then stripped the bedding ready for washing. When she went downstairs, Ben had put two mugs of strong coffee on the table and was steadily munching through a pile of warmed rolls with heather honey as he read the sports section of the Sunday paper.

Relieved he was letting her take the coward's way out of facing him, Kirsty sat down at the table, buttered herself a roll and took the news section. She glanced at him covertly a couple of times over top of the newspaper. Why had she never noticed how gorgeous his hands were? Well shaped, with long, strong fingers that felt…

Stop right there, she told herself crossly. You're not supposed to be thinking about what he did with those hands last night. Annoyed with herself, she tried to concentrate on the news.

She looked so serious, Ben thought as he watched her covertly over the top of the newspaper. Calm and graceful and very, very serious. No one would ever imagine that this woman had spiralled out of control in his arms the previous night. He wondered how she'd looked then. Had her eyes flashed gold fire? What did her face look like when it was flushed with passion?

Stop right there, he told himself. The light was off and there's no way you're going to repeat what happened, let alone repeat it with the lights on. And he buried himself back in the rugby reports.

'Good morning,' Morag greeted them as she walked into the kitchen. 'I saw Ellen McAllister at church. She asked me to tell you how grateful she was to both of you.'

'Nothing to be grateful about, Gran. We didn't save him,' Ben said quietly.

'His time had come,' Morag said simply. 'But you did all you could—and you waited for her at the hospital. She appreciated that.'

Bon nodded grimly. 'I'll pop in and see her before we go.'

Kirsty was about to add, Me too, when she realised that this was the perfect opportunity to talk to Morag and find out the truth about her condition.

But then Morag pre-empted any plans. 'Ellen won't be there. She's going down to Newcastle to pick Andy up.'

'Should she be driving?' Ben asked.

'No, but she's from tough stock and she says it makes

her feel better that she's actually doing something, not waiting around for things to happen.' Morag was matter-of-fact. 'Now, do you two want to get some fresh air before lunch? You both look as if you need it.'

Kirsty flushed to the roots of her hair. Was it so obvious what she and Ben had been doing, last night? 'I—er…'

Ben came to her rescue. 'Thanks, Gran. We're both used to late nights at work, but I suppose the travelling hasn't helped.'

'What time's your flight?'

'Four.'

'So you need to check in at three—I'll have lunch ready for one,' Morag said.

'We'll do the washing up first,' Kirsty offered.

'You'll do no such thing, young lady. Off with the pair of you,' Morag directed.

'Never argue with a Scots granny. They're always right,' Ben said wryly. He stood up, stretched, then drew Kirsty to her feet and slid his arm round her shoulder. 'Come on. See you in a bit, Gran.'

It was colder than the previous day, cold enough for them both to need warm jackets. To Kirsty's relief, he dropped his arm from her shoulders as soon as they left the house. Having his arm round her was torture, because she knew he didn't mean it. At least, not in the way she wanted him to mean it.

She just hoped that he hadn't guessed how she felt.

And it seemed as if she was a better actress than she thought, because Ben gave her a guided tour of the village, showing her where he'd gone to school and taking her round the tiny church where he'd been christened. A church much like the one she'd imagined the previous evening, its plainness showing the sheer beauty of the ancient building.

'The forest's something else,' he said as they headed out of the village and into the woods above it. 'There used to be hundreds of red squirrels scampering around all over the place. But, even better...' He left the tantalising promise hanging in the air, refusing to be drawn about the surprise he clearly had planned.

And then she saw it. A carpet of bluebells, stretching as far as she could see. The flowers were all shades of blue, verging through into lilac and even into pink. 'It's beautiful,' she said.

'Like a loch within the forest. I remember my dad—' He stopped abruptly.

Kirsty knew not to push. Ben rarely spoke about his parents. She knew that his father had died young and assumed that Ben's mother had died soon after, as he'd gone to live with Morag when he was five. Even now, it clearly still hurt him too much to talk about his mother, because Kirsty had never once heard him speak about her.

'Hey. It's OK,' she said softly, taking his hand and squeezing it.

Why on earth had he brought her here? Here, to his special place, the place his father had shown him the year before he'd died, the place Ben always went to think? Now he'd always associate the place with Kirsty, too. And the way she was holding his hand... It was almost as if she knew. Knew how he was feeling, understood—just letting him know that she cared, that she was there for him.

And she did care for him.

Just as friends.

All the same, he didn't release her hand. Worse still, he laced his fingers through hers and continued walking through the forest hand in hand with her.

They found a clear stream that was narrow enough for them both to step over; and Kirsty exclaimed in delight when she found a patch of tiny, sweet-smelling violets. 'I know you're not supposed to pick them, but your gran would love them,' she said wistfully.

'She'd love them more in the forest,' Ben told her gently, tightening the pressure of his fingers against hers.

Sensible. He was being sensible. So why didn't he just stop holding her hand? Because, he told himself, he was still shocked about Marty. It was a need for comfort, nothing more, that made him want to hold her hand like this.

Eventually they went back to the cottage, where the chicken casserole smelt wonderful. The light, fluffy mashed potato and swede Morag served with it—'You can't possibly come to Scotland without tasting neeps and tatties!' as she put it—was gorgeous, complementing the spring greens and the mustard-based sauce of the casserole.

Kirsty only just managed pudding—Morag's home-made ice cream, made with raspberries and cream from the local organic dairy, with tiny crunchy honey biscuits—and sat back with a sigh of contentment. 'I could quite happily curl up and go to sleep,' she admitted. 'You know, lazy Sunday afternoons.'

'Except we've got a plane to catch,' Ben reminded her.

'Then I'll make a start on the washing-up.'

'No, you won't,' Morag said. 'I'll do it after you've gone.'

'I'll do it, then,' Ben said, clearly guessing what Kirsty intended to do.

'The same goes for you, young man,' Morag informed him. She remained adamant—quashing any hopes Kirsty had of talking to the old lady and finishing their conversation about her health.

It seemed, Kirsty thought, that she'd have to do it by phone, when she was back in Southbay.

Finally, they took their leave of Morag and Ben drove them back to Inverness. Kirsty tried not to close her eyes this time—he'd already proved over the weekend that he was a careful driver, pulling into the passing places and managing to avoid the deer that wandered onto the road, too. And, because Ben clearly wasn't in the mood for talking, she ended up watching the loch.

'Did you see it?' Ben enquired as they reached the first suburbs of Inverness.

'What?'

'Nessie,' he teased.

'No.'

'Maybe next time.'

Except there wouldn't be a next time—would there?

CHAPTER EIGHT

MONDAY morning saw life back to normal. Kirsty was on a late and Ben was on an early, so she did the supermarket run before she went to work and whizzed round with the vacuum cleaner, leaving Ben a note under the salt-cellar to say it was his turn to clean the bathroom.

On her way in to work, she thought about the engagement plan. She'd kept her part of the bargain: she'd convinced Morag that her grandson had settled down. But did she really want Ben to keep his part of the deal? As soon as word leaked out that Kirsty was engaged to Ben Robertson—and, given how efficient the grapevine was at Jimmy's, that wouldn't take long—there would be a lot of coolness underlying the congratulations. Most of the single women in the hospital had set their sights on Ben, even the ones that hadn't thought about it, whether they admitted it or not! She really didn't want a miserable working environment with everyone disliking her. On the other hand, she already felt as if she'd got that, with the Chambers situation. And if Ben's theory was right and the engagement ring kept the consultant surgeon off her back…

In the end, she decided to leave the ring where it was rather than slide it onto the chain round her neck. And it took Jenny all of forty seconds to spot it when Kirsty set foot on the ward.

'Kirsty Brown, is that what I think it is?'

'Um—what?' Kirsty asked, playing for time.

'Left hand, ring finger, huge rock?' the surgical ward sister said meaningfully, tapping her own finger.

'Ye-es.'

'Who?'

Kirsty held her breath.

'Who?' Jenny demanded again.

'Ben,' Kirsty muttered.

'Ben, as in *your* Ben? *Ben Robertson?*'

'Uh-huh.'

Jenny's shriek of delight brought the rest of the nursing staff running. Two minutes later, the whole ward knew that Kirsty was engaged to Ben and everyone in sight was congratulating her. Just as Kirsty had suspected, a couple of the younger members of staff were rather cool towards her, but most people seemed genuinely pleased for her.

'Might I enquire what all the fuss is about?' an icy voice said behind them.

'Our Kirst flew up to Scotland this weekend and got engaged,' Jenny said, her smile daring Chambers to rain on Kirsty's parade.

'Indeed.' His gaze met Kirsty's, but she refused to quail under it. 'Remember that this is a surgical ward. Patients need quiet to recuperate from surgery. And I trust you're not going to wear your ring in Theatre, Brown.'

'Of course not.' It was on the tip of her tongue to add a sarcastic 'sir', but she resisted. Just.

'As long as you observe hygiene precautions.'

Who did he think she was, a wet-behind-the-ears first-year med student? 'Of course,' she said sweetly.

At least he didn't ask who she'd got engaged to, she thought with relief. Unless he thought she'd made it up. Well, he'd find out soon enough. She and Ben were officially engaged. And no one else needed to know that it was a fake engagement. 'I'll get scrubbed up,' she said, removing her ring and placing it on a chain around her neck.

'Do that, Brown.' Chambers spun round on his heel and stalked off.

'Is that man always so rude to you?' Jenny asked.

'Yes,' Kirsty said simply. 'But leave it, Jen. I might try getting a transfer elsewhere.'

'A and E, perhaps?' the nurse suggested with a grin.

'You never know.'

Almost as if on cue, Kirsty's pager went. She glanced at the display. 'A and E. I'd better ring and find out what they want.'

'I'll tell Sweetness and Light where you are, if he grumps in here after you,' Jenny said.

'Thanks.' Kirsty rang the number on her pager. 'Kirsty Brown—you paged me?'

'I've got a real lulu of an accident for you,' Ben said. 'Sorry, but it's a sooner rather than later.'

'I'll be down.' She replaced the receiver and left the ward, obeying her training to walk swiftly rather than run.

'So what's the story?' she asked Ben when she arrived.

'Josh Blake, aged twelve. Decided to skip school so he could mess about in the park on his skateboard with his mates. Showed off and came a cropper. Unfortunately, he landed on a railing. They managed to cut most of the railing away, but there's some left embedded. We've done X-rays and it's dangerously close to a lung.' He drew her over to the light-box and showed her the X-rays.

She whistled. 'We need that out, fast.'

Ben swiftly filled her in on the details of the pain relief he'd given the boy and the checks he'd already done. 'Blood's being cross-matched.'

'Has anyone paged an anaesthetist?'

Ben nodded. 'Ten minutes and he'll meet you in Theatre Six.'

'Thanks. Parents?'

'On their way. I'll talk to them as soon as they come in.'

'Right. Let's get him prepped. I'd better ring Jen and let her know what I'm doing.' She hoped she didn't end up talking to Chambers. Right now, she didn't have time to argue with him when a child's life needed saving—

and, knowing Chambers, he'd want to argue the point and bang on about priorities. Fine in its place, but right now wasn't the place.

'I'll do it. It'll save you time,' Ben offered.

'You're an angel.' She beamed gratefully at him. 'I'd better be off.'

'Kirsty, have you got a second?' Nina, one of the senior nurses on A and E, came into the cubicle as Kirsty was about to leave.

'Sure.' As long it was really only a second.

'I believe congratulations are in order.'

Did the grapevine at Jimmy's *really* work that fast? Kirsty wondered. 'Thank you,' she said quietly.

'You know, the pair of you have just broken about a million hearts,' Nina continued. 'But congrats anyway.'

'Thanks, Nina.' Ben smiled at her. 'I'll get the cream cakes in later, OK?'

'And you'd better make them big ones,' she retorted, laughing. 'I'll leave you to it. Just wanted to say wish you both the best, that's all.'

Ben cast Kirsty a rueful glance. 'So how long have you been in?'

'It took Jenny less than a minute to notice,' she told him.

'What about Chambers?'

'Gave me a lecture on hygiene.' She shrugged. 'You paged me before I went into Theatre. And I'm about to be busy for the rest of the afternoon, thanks to you, so he won't be able to nag me until teatime at least.'

'If he lays a finger on you—'

'I'll be fine, Ben.' She wrinkled her nose at him. 'See you later.'

Ten minutes later, she was scrubbed up and ready to operate. Joe Marinelli, the anaesthetist, was waiting for her by the patient. 'All ready when you are,' he said, his eyes crinkling to show the smile his mask hid.

'Cheers, Joe.'

'Hey—I hear you're finally doing the decent thing by Ben. Congratulations.'

'Don't you mean, he's doing the decent thing by me?'

'I know exactly what I mean, Kirsty Brown.' He winked at her.

She nodded, and turned to her patient. Adrenaline made the back of her neck prickle; the first incision always made her feel nervous and wired. And then the years of practice took over and she worked confidently, quickly yet surely, removing the railing and repairing the damage it had left behind.

It was a long, long, afternoon, but a satisfying one, Kirsty thought as she finished closing, her stitches neat and even. Although the operation itself had been delicate work, there hadn't been any extra problems with the patient going into shock on the table, worrying blood-pressure changes or heart arrhythmias. 'Let's hope he chooses the pitch for his next skateboarding practice a bit more carefully,' she said lightly. 'And does it out of school hours, too.'

She headed back to the surgical ward, but Jenny didn't have time to warn her before Chambers marched to the door of his office and barked, 'Brown, my office—now.'

Jenny sent her a sympathetic glance and Kirsty did as she was told, the euphoria she always felt after a successful operation fading swiftly.

'Why didn't you tell me where you were going?' Chambers demanded. 'I had to hear third-hand that you were operating. You're supposed to check with me first.'

'I'm sorry, there wasn't time. I needed to operate,' Kirsty explained carefully. 'But the A and E registrar called you.'

'Left a message, actually,' Chambers said crisply. 'That might have been the way you worked with Tony, but not with me. Understood?'

'Yes, sir.'

His eyes flashed, as if he'd detected sarcasm in her muted 'sir'. 'I had to delay two operations because you weren't here.'

Considering he'd treated her as a spare part rather than a useful colleague since the moment she'd dared to rebuke him for groping her, Kirsty rather doubted that. Though she'd already learned not to challenge the consultant when he was in this sort of mood. Let him bluster and it'll blow over more quickly, she told herself.

'I'm sorry,' she said, hoping the apology would pacify him.

'And I expect your private life not to interfere with your work,' he continued.

'It won't.'

'Wasn't the A and E registrar who paged you your fiancé?'

Was he implying that Ben had phoned her for social reasons, not work? Annoyance made her voice crisp. 'He was simply doing his job—the X-rays showed we needed to operate on the patient immediately.'

'Next time, he calls me, not you. Do I make myself clear?'

'Yes.'

'You'd better take a break,' Chambers said coldly. 'We'll have to slot in some extra time tomorrow. There's the ward rounds to do, bloods to be ordered.'

Bloods were usually the task of the new house officers, not the registrars, but this was clearly his way of rebuking her. Anything for a quiet life, she thought, deciding not to argue the point. 'I'll grab a sandwich and be straight back up here.'

'Good.'

Kirsty turned on her heel and walked out of his office, repressing her urge to tell him where to stick his job. She marched down the stairs to the staff canteen and, after taking one look at the curled edges of the sandwiches, abandoned the idea in favour of a couple of bits of fruit, a yoghurt and a carton of freshly squeezed orange juice. She was paying for her meal when Nina and one of her colleagues accosted her.

'You're a dark horse, Kirsty Brown. All these years you protested you and our Ben were just best mates…' Babs teased.

'We are—*were*,' Kirsty corrected herself.

'And you sneaked off to Scotland to get engaged. You don't think you're going to get away with it, do you?' Nina asked.

'I'd love to discuss this with you—really, I would—but I have to get back to the ward.' She only just stopped herself telling them what a swine Chambers was. The last thing she needed was for the grapevine to pick it up, however well meaning, and Chambers to accuse her of blackening his name.

'That why you're eating barely enough to keep a sparrow alive?' Babs asked with a meaningful look at Kirsty's lunch. 'Or is that what love does to you?'

'You know how it is,' Kirsty prevaricated.

'Well, the least you can do is buy us all a drink. Tomorrow night, eight o'clock, the Coach and Horses. Both of you. With glad rags on. Or we'll be round to collect you,' Nina informed her.

'Bully,' Kirsty retorted with a grin.

'Eight o'clock,' Nina repeated. 'And don't let him make you late.'

'I won't,' she promised.

When Kirsty finally got home that evening, Ben was already out. There were no messages under the salt-cellar, but the smell of bleach and the gleaming bathroom attested to the fact he'd read her note from that morning. She took a long bath, topping up the water several times and only getting out when the pads of her fingers were distinctly prune-like. Ben still wasn't back by the time she'd finished her book and headed for bed; she suppressed the tiny murmurs of jealousy. It was none of her business who Ben went out with, was it?

The next day, they were both on early; Ben was up first, and by the time she'd showered he'd already made a pot of coffee and was munching his way through an enormous bowl of muesli.

'Did Nina see you yesterday afternoon?' she asked as she made herself some toast.

He nodded. 'We should have guessed they wouldn't let us get away with it.' He filched a slice of toast from her plate before she could slap his hand away. 'Still, one drink won't hurt.'

Except it wasn't one drink.

When they arrived at the Coach and Horses, expecting the bar to be full of their colleagues, the place was almost deserted. Apart from Nina and Babs, who sat there with less-than-innocent smiles.

'What's going on?' Ben asked with narrowed eyes.

'Nothing. We asked you to meet us for a drink.' Mischief danced in Babs's blue eyes.

'You said buy you *all* a drink,' Kirsty reminded them.

Nina and Babs exchanged a glance. 'Never try to get something past a surgeon. All right, we're in here. Come this way,' Nina said.

Ben and Kirsty stopped dead in the entrance to the function room.

'How on earth did you manage all *this* in the space of one day?' Kirsty asked. A function room, a buffet, a band and all the staff from A and E and Surgical who weren't on duty. Except, she thought with relief, Guy Chambers. He was the last person who'd congratulate her—unless he thought it meant she'd give up her job within weeks.

'Tuesdays are always dead, so the function room wasn't booked. Mandy was on a half-day so she did the whip-round and the food run, and her mum helped her with the buffet. Teresa's cousin sings in a band so she rang him.'

Nina shrugged. 'Anyway, you know us. Always up for a party.'

'Yeah, but this…'

'C'mon, you didn't think we'd let Dr Charming go without a proper send-off?' Babs teased.

Ben coughed. 'Do you mind?'

Kirsty dug him in the ribs. 'Everyone's called you that since med school. You ought to be used to it by now.'

'Hmm.' Ben rolled his eyes. 'Well, I'd better go and see Brian and tell him I'll pick up the drinks bill.'

'*We'll* pick up the bill,' Kirsty corrected.

The evening passed in a blur of congratulations and dancing. And then there was a hush as the band stopped playing and Nina took the microphone.

'Just in case they decide to do the wedding on the sly as well,' she said, 'we thought that Ben and Kirsty ought to do the first dance in advance.'

'But—I can't dance,' Kirsty said, panicking. And the first dance, on their own, in front of everyone, as if they were madly-in-love newlyweds… They couldn't do this!

'I don't think we've got a choice,' Ben said wryly, pulling her to her feet. The band started playing a slow, romantic number. 'Follow my lead,' he whispered, 'and I'll forgive you in advance for bruising my toes.'

And then they were dancing, cheek to cheek, with Ben's arms holding her close and everyone watching them.

'Relax,' he murmured in her ear. 'You're doing fine.'

She moved her head, intending to glare at him, but he moved at the same time and somehow his mouth brushed hers. Lightly, softly, the briefest possible contact. Her body reacted instantly, reminding her how he'd made her feel when he'd made love to her. He remembered, too, she realised, as the arm round her tightened.

'Ben,' she breathed, and then he was kissing her properly, exploring her mouth in a way that made her knees go weak; if he hadn't been holding her, she would have fallen to the floor. Her hands were wrapped round his neck, her fingers tangled in his silky hair, and...

And everyone in the room was cheering, whistling and clapping.

Horrified, she pulled back slightly, and Ben broke the kiss.

She realised that he was shaking as much as she was. His mouth was swollen and his hair was mussed, and she'd have bet huge sums that she looked even worse.

'Ben, I...'

The tiny, almost imperceptible shake of his head silenced her. His eyes were unfathomable in the dimmed lighting, and Kirsty started to panic. What on earth had she—had *they*—just done? Her mouth dried. Scotland had been excusable—they'd both been reacting to the events of the day. Tonight, there was no good reason.

'Don't you ever dare claim again that you two are just best friends,' Jenny said when they escaped from the dance floor. 'That was virtually X-rated!'

Kirsty flushed deeply, and Jenny's smile softened. 'Hey, I'm pleased for you. We all are. It couldn't happen to a nicer couple.'

Except they weren't a couple. They were lying to even more people, and this whole situation was getting completely out of control. Tonight, after the party, she'd tell Ben that this all had to stop. Right now. They'd tell the truth to Morag and—well, the way things were going with Chambers, she'd end up leaving the hospital anyway, so everyone could just assume that she'd deserted Ben for a new job. He'd get plenty of offers of consolation.

So why did that thought make her feel even more miserable?

'Have a drink,' Jenny said, pressing a glass of wine into Kirsty's hand.

Kirsty expected Ben to drop his arm from her shoulders then, but he didn't. He stayed with her for the rest of the evening, keeping her close to him. And he kept his arm round her shoulders when they walked home.

'Ben, no one's about. You don't have to play the concerned fiancé any more,' Kirsty told him quietly.

'I know,' he said, but he didn't move his arm.

Her heartbeat speeded up. He knew. So why was he still…? He'd had too much to drink, she decided.

She was shivering by the time Ben unlocked the front door. And shivering even more when he closed the door behind them and pulled her into his arms.

'Ben, we—' she began.

'Not now, Kirst,' he said, and bent his head.

CHAPTER NINE

THIS wasn't her bed. Her pillowcases had soft pastel designs, not uncompromisingly masculine geometric patterns in deep colours. Her bed was single, not double. And her bed most definitely didn't contain another person.

Kirsty swallowed hard. How could she have been so stupid? Once—well, a one-off she could excuse. But why, why, why had she let Ben carry her up to his bed last night?

Mainly because she hadn't been able to help herself. Once he'd started kissing her, once his hand had slid underneath her shirt and stroked past the lace of her bra to her swelling breasts beneath, she'd been lost. Remembering what it had felt like the first time Ben had made love with her—when he'd taught her how much she'd missed.

This time round, it had been even better. She'd matched him kiss for kiss, touch for touch. And now she was lying in his arms, a trail of her clothes leading from his bed all the way down the stairs…

Oh, Kirsty, you fool, she thought. You utter, utter fool. This wouldn't last. It couldn't. They'd have three weeks at most: that was as long as Ben's relationships ever lasted. She should have just told him no, kept him at arm's length.

And then Ben kissed the nape of her neck. 'Good morning.'

'Ben. I—um…'

'Mmm.' His hand slid lower, nudging between her thighs, and she was powerless to resist. 'You feel good, Kirsty. Soft and warm and…mmm.' He nuzzled the skin

103

on her shoulder. 'You smell nice, too.' He touched the tip of his tongue to her skin. 'And taste good.'

'We shouldn't—'

He pulled her closer, so she could feel his arousal. 'We're both on a late today. It's eight-thirty. Which means we have three whole hours before we have to even think about getting up,' he murmured sinfully into her ear.

Kirsty pulled her last remaining shreds of sense together. 'We can't—'

He cheated. Because he didn't argue; he simply turned her round to face him, rubbed the tip of his nose against hers and kissed her.

By the time she was capable of thought again, they'd made love twice and Ben had gone downstairs—wearing absolutely nothing—to fix them some coffee.

She should get up. Now. Have a cold shower to shock some sense back into her. Except if Ben heard the shower running, he was more than capable of turning the heat back up. Or letting his body turn the temperature up for them until she was oblivious of the freezing water as he soaped her skin, lifted her up and—

'I think it'd have to be a platinum penny for them,' Ben said, amusement lilting his voice as he put two mugs of coffee on his bedside cabinet.

Kirsty flushed and tried to hide under the covers.

'What were you thinking about just then? Tell me.' His voice dropped an octave, all husky and sexy, and desire burned in the pit of her stomach.

'No.'

He ripped the duvet off her and gave her a truly wicked smile, the sort that melted her bones. 'Kirsty Brown, do I have to *make* you tell me?'

The best part of an hour later, she ended up taking their stone-cold coffees downstairs and making a fresh pot. Except she was fully dressed—after a very hasty shower, taken alone—and she waited downstairs for Ben rather than risk taking the coffee back to bed. Absently, she ate a slice of toast.

'Hi,' he said softly as he walked into the kitchen.

That smile. Why had she ever thought herself immune to it? Ben Robertson was gorgeous, from those irrepressible curls and incredible eyes right down to his perfectly formed toes. 'Hi, yourself,' she returned shyly.

'Toast, hmm?' He bent down to lick a crumb from the corner of her lip. 'And heather honey, if I'm not mistaken.'

'Ben, we—'

'I know. We're due in at work.' He stared at her mouth. 'Though, right now, I'm sorely tempted to ring in sick.' He smiled—just. 'Except I know your sense of duty's too strong to let me.'

'I don't exactly feel like "Sensible Kirst" right now,' she admitted. 'Ben, this thing between us...'

'Don't ask me. I can't explain it either.' He topped up her mug, then poured himself a coffee. 'Kirst, I don't want to lie to you. *Especially* you,' he added. 'You know I can't make any promises.'

Pain squeezed through every pore. He could still say that, after what they'd shared?

'Maybe it's a phase and we'll grow out of it. Think of this as—oh, an extension of our friendship.'

'An extension of our friendship?' she repeated in disbelief.

He made a face. 'Sorry, Kirst. That sounded bad. I didn't mean to make it sound cheap. It isn't. You mean a lot to me—you know that.'

'Uh-huh,' she managed. What had she expected—a declaration of love?

'The last thing I want is to hurt you, but I can't give you white lace and promises. I can't give *anyone* white lace and promises,' he said sombrely. 'It's just the way I am.'

'So what do we do now?'

'I don't know. I don't want to lose you, Kirst.'

'I don't want to lose you either.'

'We're going to be late for work,' he said. 'Let's talk about this later.'

Coward, she thought. But, then, she was just as bad, because she didn't press the point.

He didn't hold her hand or put his arm round her on the way to Jimmy's, and he kept the conversation very firmly in the area of shop talk. They parted at the hospital entrance as casually as always, but Kirsty couldn't stop thinking of the way it had felt to wake up in his arms that morning. Or the way they'd made love. So much so that she actually contaminated her hands after she'd scrubbed and had to start all over again. She also dropped a retractor, earning her a well-deserved rebuke from Chambers.

'Kirsty, what's got into you?' Paul Fisher asked later in the locker room.

She very nearly corrected him—who, not what—and flushed scarlet at what she'd almost blurted out.

'Kirsty?'

'Nothing. I'm still focused a hundred per cent on my job.'

Paul grinned. 'You don't have to tell *me* that. I'm your junior. It's just that…you're different today.'

Yeah. I woke up in the arms of the man I love.

No. She shouldn't be in love with Ben. He didn't do relationships. And he wouldn't make an exception for her—he'd already told her as much. Falling in love with Ben would be the most stupid thing she could do.

And she had a nasty feeling she'd already done it.

'I think,' Paul said, 'you need caffeine. Lots of it.'

'I've got notes to write up.'

'They'll wait.'

She smiled. 'Thanks. You're a sweetie. But they won't wait.' Not if she wanted to retrieve the situation with Chambers. He'd zoom in on the fact that she'd neglected part of her job, and she had no intention of giving him the opportunity to put her on disciplinary.

'I'll bring one in to you, then,' Paul said. 'On condition you give me those references about stapling rather than stitching an anastomosis.'

'Deal.'

When Kirsty finally got a break, an hour before the end of her shift, Ben was already in the cafeteria. With another woman. The usual type—tall, slim, long blonde hair, with the kind of natural-looking make-up that took hours to apply. She was gazing adoringly at him, hanging on his every word, and Ben was clearly being Dr Charming, focusing on her and making her feel important. Kirsty had seen him doing that dozens of times, so she ignored the stab of jealousy. It was probably business, she told herself. The woman was probably new in A and E, or a drug rep, or something like that.

Ha. Who was she trying to kid?

But even if it wasn't business, Kirsty didn't have any claim on Ben. The diamond solitaire on the chain round her neck was…well, convenient, for both of them. Nothing more. Forget it, she thought, and found herself a quiet corner of the cafeteria where she didn't have to look at him being sweet to another woman.

Though clearly he'd seen her because, when she was morosely stirring the sugar she didn't usually take into her latte, she heard a chair scrape next to her and looked up.

'Hi,' he said.

'Hi, yourself.'

'Didn't you see me?'

'You looked busy.'

'Selina, you mean? She's a liaison officer from the local college. She wants me to give a careers talk to their sixth-formers about life in A and E. You should have come over.'

'Why?'

'Because you could do a talk, too. About surgery. Prove to the girls that women really can make it through the system.' To her horror, he leaned over and kissed her. *Kissed her.* In front of everyone in the cafeteria. 'You're having a bad day, aren't you?'

'Mmm.'

'Forget the coffee.'

'What?'

'Come with me, Dr Brown.'

No. All she had to do was say no. But the twinkle in those gorgeous blue eyes was irresistible. She left her coffee and let him lead her down a corridor.

'Where are we going?'

'You'll see.' He did a quick check, then opened a door, switched on a light and pulled her inside.

'This is a linen cupboard!' she hissed.

'I know.' He started unbuttoning her tunic top beneath her white coat.

'Ben, we c—' she began, but the negative turned into a soft sigh of pleasure as he stroked her hardening nipples.

'I've been thinking about you all day,' he said. 'You, me…and this.' He replaced his fingers with his mouth and she gasped.

When he lifted his head again, they were both flushed.

'I need you, Kirst,' he said rawly.

Need wasn't the same as love. She should just walk away, right now. But she couldn't. Not when he was looking at her like that. She'd never known how *hot* blue eyes could seem, blazing with desire. Helplessly, she opened her arms, and he lifted her up against the door, the combined weight of their bodies guaranteed to hold it shut. He kissed her again as he removed her trousers and entered her, his mouth swallowing her cry of pleasure. And then time stopped until she was in free-fall, her body convulsing round his. She was still shuddering when he withdrew. He supported her until she could stand on her own two feet again, then smiled and kissed the tip of her nose.

'Ben…'

'You're turning into a shameless hussy. I know.' His eyes glittered. 'I rather like it.'

'We're at *work*!'

'On a break,' he pointed out.

'We really, really—'

'Must do this again some time. I quite agree, Dr Brown. Liaison meetings between A and E and Surgical are very important.'

She aimed a slap at him. 'Stop twisting my words!'

His eyes crinkled at the corners. 'As if I'd dare.'

She still couldn't quite believe what they'd just done—made love in the linen cupboard.

It was as if he could read her mind. 'I'll let you into a secret,' he said huskily. 'I've never done this before either.'

Before she had time to digest that, he restored order to her clothes and combed her hair with his fingers. 'That's better. You look respectable again now.'

She didn't feel respectable. And supposing someone saw them coming out of the cupboard?

Either he'd definitely become a mind-reader, or her thoughts were written all over her face, because he smiled again and eased the door open. 'Coast's clear. You go first, I'll follow in a couple of minutes.'

Crazy. This whole thing was absolutely crazy and she knew it was all going to end in tears. But Kirsty had a smile on her face as she returned to the surgical ward.

Ben was still with patients when Kirsty's shift ended, so she walked home alone. She glanced at her watch. Morag was probably still in. Just. So if she rang now, before Ben came home, she might just get to the bottom of Morag's secret.

Morag answered at the fourth ring. 'Hello?'

'Morag, it's Kirsty.'

'How are you?'

'Fine. And you?'

'Oh, I'm fine, I'm fine.' Kirsty could imagine Morag's hand flapping in impatience.

'Ben's at work right now,' Kirsty said. Which made this the perfect moment to ask. 'Actually, Morag, I really need to talk to you.'

'What about?'

'That conversation we started having in your kitchen.'

'Can't remember, lass. When you get to my age, you forget.'

That wasn't true, Kirsty knew. Not much got past Morag Robertson. But if that was the way she wanted to play it… 'Morag, you know that Ben's convinced himself that you're at death's door, don't you?'

'Don't be silly. He's *seen* me. I'm perfectly all right.'

'Are you really, Morag? Look, you can trust me. I won't pass on anything you don't want to tell him until you're ready.'

'I'm fine. Look, I've got to go.'

Before Kirsty could protest, the line went dead. She sighed and replaced the receiver. No wonder Ben was so worried about Morag. It was too suspicious. Her refusal to discuss things and her continued insistence that she was fine could only mean one thing—that she was seriously ill and didn't want Ben to know because she didn't want him to worry. The ironic thing was that Ben would worry less if he *did* know the truth because at least he'd know what was going on.

Somehow, she had to persuade Morag to tell her the truth.

Still brooding, she walked upstairs and ran herself a bath. She'd just settled into the water when she heard Ben's key in the front door. It took him about two minutes to work out where she was, and then he knocked on the bathroom door.

'Can I come in?'

He didn't wait for an answer but walked in, carrying a bottle of Merlot, one glass and a tin of cannoli wafers.

'One glass?' she asked breathlessly.

'I thought we'd share it.' He looked up at the bathroom light and wrinkled his nose. 'Too bright,' he said, and left the room. A few moments later, he was back with a large church candle and a box of matches. He balanced the candle-holder on the window-sill, lit the candle and turned the overhead light off. 'That's more like it.'

'Hang on, this is *my* bath you're commandeering,' Kirsty said.

'Ours,' he corrected.

Her mouth went dry as he stripped off in front of her, completely unselfconscious. All the times she'd seen him nearly naked in the past on hot summery days in the garden, and she'd never really noticed how strong and powerful his body was, how long and well shaped his legs were, how…

She stopped thinking as he climbed in opposite her, taking the tap end.

He took one of the cannoli wafers from the tin and bit off one end, clearly savouring the crispness of the wafer against the smoothness of the chocolate and hazelnut praline filling.

'Where's mine?' she asked.

'Same as the glass. We'll share it.' He held the wafer out to her, making her lean forward to take a bite. They took it in turns, bite for bite, until there was only a tiny piece left. He placed it between her lips, then leaned forward to bite his half from her lips. And then Kirsty was only aware of the swish of water as he dragged her onto his lap and she wrapped her legs round his waist. She rocked against him, teasing him. When he lifted her slightly so he could enter her, she stopped thinking and arched her back, matching him thrust for thrust.

'I can't get you out of my head,' Ben told her huskily as he wrapped her in a soft towelling bath-sheet, still warm from being hung over the radiator. 'I was thinking about you all the way home tonight.'

'Oh, yes?'

'Mmm-hmm. I thought you'd already be working. The way you usually do, lying on your bed with one leg kicked back behind you, playing with the ends of your hair while you read.'

He noticed what she did in *that* much detail?

'And I was going…' he nuzzled her cheek '…to stop you overdoing it.'

'How?' She blurted the word out.

He gave her a lazy, very sexy smile. 'Easy. I was going to pick you up and take you to my room.'

'Oh, yes?' Her voice grew husky again at the thought.

'Mmm-hmm.' He nibbled her earlobe. 'Sleep with me tonight, Kirst. I want to go to sleep in your arms. I want to hear your heart beating as I fall asleep. And I want your face to be the first thing I see when I wake up.'

This was as near as Ben would get to a declaration of love, she thought sadly. Or did he say that to all his women?

'Kirst?'

He sounded very unsure, and she realised that she'd tensed in his arms. She wriggled one arm free from the bath-sheet and stroked his face. 'OK.'

His eyes blazed and he lifted her up and carried her to his bed. Much, much later, he retrieved the wine and the cannoli wafers from the bathroom and fed her with alternate sips and bites. And at last they settled so he could sleep in her arms, his head resting on her breast so he could hear her heartbeat.

I love you, she thought as she stroked his hair. Right now, you're like a little boy wanting comfort from a nightmare—and I'm the only one who can give you what you need. And maybe that's the truth. Maybe love's what you need to heal you. And I'm the one to give it to you.

*   *   *

During the next couple of weeks, Kirsty began to believe that she'd found what she'd been looking for all her life. True happiness. At work, life was fine. Chambers was as snappy as ever, questioning her judgement and treating her as if she was far less qualified than she was, but his barbs didn't hurt her the way they had. Every day, it felt as if the sun was shining—even on the days when it absolutely poured down and everyone arrived at work moaning that they were soaked. Kirsty smiled through it all, because she had Ben.

She hadn't slept in her own room since the night of their second engagement party. She still used her own room for studying, on the nights when Ben was working a late when she was on early or the nights he was out playing in the hospital squash league, but he always came in to collect her. And he carried out the promise he'd made earlier, marking her page with a piece of paper then picking her up and carrying her to his room, before making passionate love with her.

Best of all, Ben seemed to have changed, too. He wasn't doing his usual thing of backing off before things became too serious. On the days when she was on late and he was on early, he brought her coffee in bed and left her little sticky notes on the toaster to make her laugh, and he left her something that only needed heating through if he was out. On the days when she was on early and he was on late, she did the same for him—and if she wasn't in Theatre he enticed her home for lunch and they ended up running to the hospital, breathless and laughing and still slightly rumpled from bed. And at night he held her so close, as if she were the most precious thing in his world and he was afraid to let her go.

Maybe, Kirsty thought, it was different this time. He'd known her for so long he knew virtually everything about her. There were no surprises in store. So maybe at last he'd let himself love. Maybe he'd let himself love her. And maybe this time it would be happy-ever-after for both of them. The smile was still on her face even as she opened her books and began to concentrate on her studies.

Ben looked at his watch. Eleven o'clock. Kirsty had been on early, surgery had overrun so she had been late finishing her shift—he knew that because he'd played squash against Paul Fisher tonight—and now she was *still* working. Her bedroom door was closed, but Ben knew exactly what she was doing. Lying facedown on the bed with a huge textbook in front of her, one leg kicked up behind her, playing with the ends of her hair as she absorbed what she was reading and occasionally made notes in the margin with a pencil.

She was pushing herself too hard again—no doubt trying to prove something to Chambers. But if she kept up this pace, she'd either collapse or make a disastrous mistake and her career would lie in tatters. In the past, he'd always stopped her getting to this point by the simple method of sliding a used envelope onto the page to mark it, closing the book and walking off with it.

Now… Things were different. That night in the bathroom he'd told her his plan for stopping her overdoing it, but now he wasn't so sure. Would she push him away if he tried to come between her and her work—even if it *was* for her own good? He rapped on her door and opened it a crack. 'Kirst?'

'Mmm?'

She was lying on the bed, just as he'd expected. Desire rippled through him. Why had he never noticed what perfect feet she had? And she'd painted her toenails lavender blue. A soft, pretty, feminine colour.

'Did you want something, Ben?'

Now he'd just made a complete idiot of himself, standing there gawping at her. 'Yes. Time to close that book, Kirst. You're on early tomorrow and you've been working since the crack of dawn.'

'I'm fine. I need to study, Ben.'

'You'll walk your exams, and you know it.' He folded his arms. Time to get tough with her. 'Kirst, you can't keep up this pace. Take a break.'

'I'm fine,' she repeated.

'You're playing into Chambers's hands. Study all night, make a mistake at work because you're too tired to do it properly, and it'll give him just the excuse he needs to stick you on disciplinary or even get rid of you,' he pointed out.

'I'm fine,' she said stubbornly.

'Right.' He filched a page from her notebook, used it to mark her place in the thick textbook and closed the book firmly.

'Ben!'

'Stop arguing.' He picked her up. 'You can work to-morrow when you've had a rest. I'll even test you, if you like. Right now, you've done enough.' Before she could argue any further, he kissed her. And kissed her. And carried her to his bed.

She was warm and soft and giving, and being with her was the best feeling on earth. Watching her face as she climaxed, the way her brown eyes turned pure gold... It gave him a kick like nothing else.

He smiled and leaned over to rub the tip of his nose against hers. 'My beautiful, wanton Kirsty.'

'Wanton?' She smiled back at him. 'You're the one who made me that way.'

'Are you accusing me of corrupting you, Dr Brown?' he teased.

Her smile broadened. 'Better than that.'

'Yeah?'

'Yeah.' She reached up to stroke his face. 'I love you, Ben.'

Love?

She'd just said it. The L word. The word that marked the beginning of the end. He went cold. No. This couldn't be happening. Not with Kirsty. He'd always thought she was safe—that was half the reason he'd dragged her into this crazy engagement of convenience in the first place. But now she was saying she loved him. Which meant commitment. Which meant he'd hurt her. Which meant...

Fingers of ice rippled up his spine and he pulled away, turning to lie on his back.

She shifted onto her side, propping herself on one elbow so she could see his face. 'Ben?'

'Sorry. I'm a bit tired. Hard day,' he said.

The look on her face told him he wasn't convincing. Not even slightly.

'Kirsty...' He took her hand. 'Look, it's not you. It's me.'

Worse and worse. He had to shut up now, before he told her they ought to cool things a bit, give themselves some time and space. Though that was what he'd tell her if he was being sensible. This whole thing was happening way too fast for him. And for her. She had her career to think about, and he...he...

'I, er, I think I'll have a shower,' Kirsty said, her voice subdued.

'Mmm-hmm.'

He didn't dare look at her as she slid from the bed. He knew what he'd see written in her face. Hurt. Rejection. Confusion.

Why couldn't he have just told her he loved her, too? He did love her. Just...not in the way she wanted it. Not the white-lace-and-promises kind of love. What he felt for Kirsty was...different. It was the friendship kind of love. Deeper than he'd ever felt for anyone else, and not having her in his life would be like not being able to see colours any more, but it wasn't the right kind of love for her.

What was he going to do? He needed to make things all right again, but he knew they could never go back to their old friendship. Not after the way things had been between them these past couple of weeks. What the *hell* was he going to do?

He found himself holding his breath as he heard the bathroom door close. Every second brought her nearer his door. How was he going to face her?

He wasn't. Because she walked right past his door, back to her own room. He heard the door close. And then he closed his eyes in utter misery, wondering just how he was going to make it up to her.

CHAPTER TEN

WHY, why, why did you have to open your big mouth? Kirsty asked herself. Things were fine between you. You were happy—*both* of you were happy. But, no, you had to assume that you were different from his usual women; you had to rush in and tell Ben you love him instead of waiting until he was ready to hear it.

She'd known it had been a mistake the moment the words were out of her mouth. That sudden, stricken look in his eyes... If she hadn't known better, she'd have said he'd actually panicked. The end result was the same. He'd backed off. He hadn't even suggested taking a shower with her. And the cold water had brought back enough of her senses to make her walk past his room to her own. She wasn't going to *beg* him to love her.

What now?

He didn't feel the same way about her, that was for sure. And the chances of going back to their old friendship was looking pretty remote. Which left...what?

They avoided each other the next morning. Kirsty skulked in her room until she heard Ben leave, then took the long way to work so she wouldn't accidentally bump into him. She took all her breaks in the surgical rest-room rather than braving the staff restaurant—no way did she want to face him in front of an audience—and she studied late at the hospital, not going home until she was sure he was likely to be out.

To her relief, he was. She made herself a scratch meal of pasta with a tuna and tomato sauce, then went to her room, turning the light out as soon as she heard the front door close. Would he come to her? She waited, breathing shallowly, but he simply took a shower and went straight to his own room without knocking on her door.

She was on early again the next morning, while he was on late and didn't come down for breakfast. There was no message for her beneath the salt-cellar, and they managed to avoid each other again at work. When the third day like that went by, Kirsty knew it was hopeless. It was over. Completely over. A world without Ben was unthinkable—but that was how her life was going to be from now on. A world where all the rainbows had dissolved, the sun had dimmed and the birds had stopped singing. Just cold, empty days stretching from here to eternity.

The thought chilled her so much that she forgot to use her kid gloves with Chambers in Theatre.

'A subtotal gastrectomy,' he said, referring to Keith Marchant, their patient with an intractable peptic ulcer. 'Which means what, Fisher?'

'Removal of a portion of the stomach, including the ulcer-bearing area and part of the parietal cell mass.'

'And why?

'It reduces the risk of the ulcer becoming malignant in the future.'

'Good.'

Even before the words were out, Kirsty knew she shouldn't have said them. 'Why not a selective vagotomy?'

'Are you questioning my judgement, Brown?'

'Just suggesting an alternative,' she said. 'If we do a resection of the vagus nerve, it'll reduce the stimulation of the gastric secretions and stop the pain.'

'And reduce the motility of the stomach, which interferes with gastric emptying,' Chambers snapped back.

Put up or shut up. But her mouth wasn't working in tandem with her brain. 'That's why Tony does a selective vagotomy—leaving part of the vagus nerve intact, especially the sections supplying the antrum.'

She'd well and truly waved the red flag: Tony. 'That might be how *Tony* did things,' Chambers rapped, 'but it isn't the way *I* do things.'

She could have retrieved the situation by suggesting that Paul needed to know all the options and maybe they should talk about pyloroplasty as well, where they surgically altered the pylorus to improve gastric emptying. But from the look in Chambers's eyes, he didn't want to turn this into a teaching case and if she said another word he'd explode. It wasn't fair on Paul—or their patient—so she subsided. Fast. And observed while Chambers did the operation *his* way.

That evening she wrote Ben a note, put it in an envelope, together with her engagement ring, and left it under the salt-cellar. Three more phone calls, and she'd set everything in motion.

I'm sorry. It's my fault. I know we can't be friends again, so I'll just wish you well for the future. I'll explain to Morag. K.

Ben read the note four times before the words sank in. Kirsty had returned his ring—and she was going to explain *what* exactly to Morag? And what did she mean, wishing him well for the future? Where was she going?

Oh, hell. He took the stairs three at a time. Kirsty's room was empty. With growing unease, he checked her wardrobe. Her overnight bag was gone. Her clothes all seemed to be there, and she might have lent the bag to someone so it didn't necessarily mean she'd gone…did it?

He checked the bathroom. Toothbrush, toothpaste, her favourite lemon-scented shower gel, shampoo… All gone. Well, maybe she'd just gone to stay with a friend overnight, just taking one change of clothes with her.

Oh, who was he trying to kid? There was only one place she could have gone, and he knew it.

He rang the airport. The flight for Inverness had left and, no, they couldn't give out passenger information.

Half an hour later, he was at the flight desk, making the request in person. 'I really need to know if my fiancée made the flight. My gran's answering machine stopped working in the middle of Kirsty's message so she doesn't know what time the flight gets in.' He was lying through his teeth, but he had to know. Had she really gone to Scotland?

Some of his desperation must have shown in his voice or his eyes, because the desk clerk took pity on him. 'The flight gets in at half past ten.'

'And Kirsty Brown was definitely on it?'

'We're not supposed to give out information like that.'

'Please?' His voice cracked.

She unbent even further. 'Yes.'

'Thank you. Thank you so much.' Ben squeezed her hand. 'Now I can go and ring my gran.'

Except Morag wasn't answering the phone. And she'd left her answering machine switched off. Ben tried every ten minutes for the next hour. Finally, he admitted defeat. If Morag had gone to meet Kirsty at the airport, she probably knew everything already. There was nothing he could do about it. And it was getting too late to ring now—he'd call in the morning then get the next flight possible.

'Kirsty, love.' Morag hugged her warmly in the doorway, then stood back to usher her inside. 'You look terrible. What's happened?'

'It's a long story,' Kirsty said quietly, putting her overnight bag down, 'and I didn't want to tell you over the phone.'

'Ben's all right?'

She nodded. 'He's fine. Just...' She took a deep breath. 'It's hard to know where to start.'

'Try the beginning.' Morag led her into the kitchen, sat

her down and switched the kettle on. 'Tea? Or do you need a tot of whisky?'

Kirsty grimaced. 'Sorry, I'm not a spirits drinker. Tea'd be lovely, thanks.'

'It must be serious for you to fly all the way up here and then get a hire car,' Morag said. 'If you'd phoned earlier I could have sent a taxi.'

'That's OK. I didn't mind driving.' Actually, she had. Driving along the lochside had been hell—she'd driven like a snail, worried that she might hit a deer, and she'd ended up pulling into a passing place several times so the impatient traffic behind her could file past. Plus, she'd been reminded of the last time she'd driven there, with Ben. In the days before she'd ruined everything.

'So what's happened?'

'I...' To her horror, Kirsty burst into tears. By the time she'd composed herself again and Morag had made them both a cup of tea, she felt hideously embarrassed. 'I'm sorry.'

'That's all right, love. Now, what's wrong?'

Kirsty ended up telling Morag the whole sorry story—how the engagement had been cooked up by Ben to stop Morag worrying about him, and how she'd agreed to help him. And how she'd made the fatal mistake of falling in love with him and telling him, so she'd ruined everything.

When she'd finished, Morag looked stricken.

'I'm sorry, Morag. I know you're ill—that's why I came up to tell you in person. I thought it'd be less of a shock for you than hearing it over the phone,' Kirsty said finally. 'Also I'm a doctor, so I'm here if you're taken ill overnight or what have you.'

'Oh, Kirsty. What have I done?'

'What have *you* done?' Kirsty repeated, not understanding.

Morag passed a shaking hand over her face. 'I'm not ill.'

'But—the angina?'

'Oh, that's nothing.' Morag flapped her hand dismissively. 'The doctor's given me tablets for that.' She bit her lip. 'I thought if Ben was worried about me, he might wake up to himself and settle down. So I let him think there was a bit more to it than that.'

'So you're all right really? Apart from the angina, that is?'

Morag nodded. 'I knew I shouldn't have done it. I always brought him up never to tell lies. When you asked me what was wrong—here and on the phone—I lost my nerve a bit. I didn't know how to tell you the truth. If I had, you wouldn't have had to hare all the way up here... Oh, I'm so sorry.'

'That's OK. I can understand why you said it. I didn't think Ben'd ever settle down either,' Kirsty admitted. 'Even his nicer girlfriends never seemed to last more than three weeks. He just didn't seem to let anyone get close.'

'Except you,' Morag pointed out.

'As his friend. I'm not even that now.'

'And you love him?'

Kirsty nodded. 'If only I hadn't told him.'

'He'd probably have guessed,' Morag said.

'And backed off anyway,' Kirsty finished. She sighed. 'I don't understand it. Why's he so scared of commitment—of love? He had a happy childhood with you.'

'Not as happy as it could have been.' Morag poured them both some more tea, and opened a tin of her home-made honey biscuits. 'His mother saw to that.'

'But she died when he was young, didn't she?'

'Is that what Ben told you?'

'No, but he never mentioned her being around after his father died. I just assumed...' Kirsty's voice faded. It looked as if Ben hadn't trusted her completely either—even in the days when they'd been close. He hadn't told her the truth about his mother. Kirsty ignored the fact that she'd been just as economical with the truth about Luke.

'Sarah couldn't cope when Ben's father died. She went

to pieces and asked me to look after the boy for a while. Then she took him back—until she met someone else. Gordon didn't want children and she wanted Gordon, so she shipped Ben back to me. He was five at the time.'

Kirsty, imagining Ben as a small, confused child, not understanding why his dad and then his mum suddenly weren't around, could have cried for him. 'But he stayed with you for good after that?'

'Though he still wanted his mum. He used to be so excited when Sarah was coming to see him for the weekend.'

'At least they had weekends together, then.'

Morag's eyes glittered. 'Precious few. Most of the time, she cancelled at the last minute. There was always some excuse—Gordon needed her to go to a function with him or there was an important dinner party. Always something. I used to ring her to remind her about Ben's birthday, but most of the time she was weeks late for it. Even his Christmas presents were late, and she always said it'd be better for me to go to parents' evening and the nativity play at school, seeing as I was bringing him up.'

Kirsty's eyes sparked orange with outrage. 'How could she *do* that to him, keep letting him down like that?'

'It's just the way she was.' Morag was phlegmatic about it, but Kirsty guessed the older woman had been angry on Ben's behalf at the time. As angry as Kirsty was now.

'Is she still alive?' Kirsty asked.

Morag nodded. 'Though Ben hasn't spoken to her since he was fourteen. She asked him to come and live with her after she divorced Gordon—but three weeks later she met someone else.'

'And sent Ben back to you again?' Kirsty guessed.

'Aye. She didn't mean to hurt him, mind. She just couldn't be the kind of mum he wanted, there for him all the time.' Morag gave a heavy sigh. 'Maybe that's why he's never settled down. Maybe he's afraid to get too close to anyone in case he's let down again. Or maybe he thinks he'll turn out like his mother and he doesn't want to hurt anyone the way he was hurt. I don't know.' She bit her lip. 'I thought with you it'd be different.'

'I'd never let him down,' Kirsty said fiercely.

'I know, dear. He knows it, too, deep down. But sometimes when you're scared you can't think logically.'

Kirsty nodded slowly. 'So where do we go from here?'

'I don't know.' The old lady's eyes glittered. 'It's something you'll have to work out between you.'

Kirsty slept badly and was sitting in Morag's kitchen early the next morning, drinking tea with her feet up by the old range cooker, when the phone rang. Not wanting the old lady to rush downstairs and risk a fall, Kirsty answered it. 'Hello?'

'Kirst? Is that you?'

She recognised his voice instantly. 'Hello, Ben.'

'Are you all right?'

'I'm fine.'

'And Gran?'

'Fine.'

'What have you told her?'

'The truth. That we never really were engaged.'

'And?'

'And she's fine, Ben. She understands.'

'But her illness…'

'You've got nothing to worry about.'

'How do you mean?'

'I'll let her tell you.'

'I'm catching the first flight up this morning.'

She could hear the panic in his voice. 'You don't need to do that. Really. She's fine.'

Gran was all right, thank God. But how was Kirsty? He couldn't tell from her voice. She had her doctor's voice on, professional and calm. Was she hurt, angry, sad? Relieved, even? Ben's throat hurt and he could hardly get the words out. 'Your note... Did you mean it?'

'Yes.'

'All of it?'

'How do you mean?'

The bit about not being friends again. Please, don't let her have meant that. 'It wasn't your fault, you know that. It was mine.' He sighed. 'I should have just left things how they were between us.'

'It's done now.'

And it can't be undone. 'Kirst, I never meant to hurt you. You were—*are*—my best friend.'

'So why didn't you tell me about your mum?'

His *mother*? Why was she asking about his mother? Ben's knuckles turned white as he gripped the receiver. What had Gran told her? 'It wasn't important.'

'Not important enough to share with me?'

'No,' he said shortly. He didn't want to discuss Sarah. Not now, not ever. She wasn't part of his life any more. 'Anyway, according to your note, you're not.'

'Not what?'

'My best friend any more.'

He was taken aback to hear her laugh. 'What's so funny?'

'You sound like a five-year-old at school. I bet your bottom lip's sticking out.'

'It's doing nothing of the kind,' he said stiffly.

'You've got your sulky voice on.'

'Now who's behaving like a five-year-old?' He paused. 'Come home, Kirst.'

'Home?'

'To Southbay.' To *me*. No. He couldn't tell her that. Sound too needy and she'd walk away—just like Sarah always had. He had to keep it light. 'We're out of clean plates and it's your turn to do the washing-up.'

'You know where the dishcloth is.'

'I miss you.' The words were out before he could stop them. Hell. He hadn't meant to tell her that. He could barely admit it to himself. 'Being around the place, I mean. It's weird not having to queue for the bathroom.'

'Maybe you ought to get a new housemate.'

'No, I'm used to you now.'

'Seriously, Ben. Maybe I should move out.'

'Don't do that, Kirst. We've been together too long.'

'Maybe that's the point,' she said sadly.

'Look, I've hurt you and I'm sorry. I told you I can't do the white-lace-and-promises bit. But I don't want to lose you,' he added for clarification.

She didn't want to lose him either. But she wasn't sure if she could cope with going back to their old relationship after what had happened between them. How could she stand watching him go out with other women when she wanted him for herself? Would this longing she had for him ever go away?

'Kirst? Are you still there?'

'I'm here,' she said softly.

'Come home. We'll sort it out, I promise. I'll keep my hands to myself. I'll even do your share of the housework for the next week.'

'Hmm.' She pretended to consider it.

'Next fortnight?'

'Make it a month and it's a deal.'

'You're a tough woman.' He paused. 'Let me know which flight you're catching. I'll meet you from the airport.'

'No need. I haven't got that much luggage.' She paused. 'I'll get your gran to call you later, OK?'

When Kirsty returned to Southbay the following evening, Ben met her at the airport. She hadn't called him with her flight details, so she guessed Morag had done it for her.

'Hi.'

'Hi, yourself.'

'Good flight?' He took her bag, ignoring her protests that she was perfectly capable of carrying her own.

'Fine. Your gran sent you some goodies.'

'She told me.' He sighed. 'And that she'd lied to me about her health.'

'A white lie, Ben,' Kirsty reminded him. 'She had your best interests at heart. And we lied to her, too.'

'I suppose that makes us quits.' He gave her a sidelong glance. 'What about us?'

'What about us?' She threw the question firmly back at him.

'Are we quits, Kirst?' At her continued silence, he added, 'What I mean is, are we still friends?'

'I suppose so.'

He smiled at her. 'It's good to have you back, best-friend Kirst.'

Best-friend Kirst. If only—if *only*—she could have been more.

CHAPTER ELEVEN

BEN was as good as his word. He kept his hands off Kirsty over the next few days and treated her like the friend she'd been for years. Though he found it harder than he'd expected. The time they'd spent together as lovers had been so short, and yet it had generated so many memories. Everything reminded him of making love with Kirsty. Honey—when he'd licked it from her lips over breakfast. Coffee—when they'd shared it in bed. Ice cream, cannoli wafers, red wine… The kitchen soon became off limits. Having a bath or shower was just as bad. And waking up alone in his bed was torture now he knew what it was like to wake up curled round her body.

It'll go away, he told himself. Because he wasn't in love with her. It was just…unrequited lust.

Though it hadn't been unrequited, had it?

It took him twenty minutes under a cold shower to stop that thought. And even then it kept sneaking back to him. Especially the time he tried the old trick of stopping Kirsty studying too hard.

Bad move, he told himself even as he walked through her door. He could still remember the last time he'd stopped her studying, by carrying her to his bed. It would be so, so easy to do that now.

But he couldn't. He shouldn't. He *mustn't*.

'Time to stop, Kirst,' he said.

She looked at him over her shoulder. How had he forgotten how delectable her rear was? And those gold lights in her eyes… Was she remembering, too, how it had been between them?

No. It wasn't part of their deal. 'You've got ten

minutes. I'll make you some hot milk. If that book's still open when I come back, I'll chuck it straight out of the window,' he said.

'Tyrant.' But at least she was smiling. Sort of.

'One hot milk with cinnamon and brown sugar coming up,' he said, and left the room before he really lost it and carried her to his bed anyway. Somehow he managed to make her a drink and took it back to her room. To his relief, she was actually putting her books away. If she'd still been lying there, he wasn't sure if he'd have been able to keep his hands off her.

He cleared this throat. 'Hot milk.'

She took the mug from him, sipped the contents and smiled. 'Thanks. This is good.'

'I'm glad you're being sensible now.'

'I'm always sensible.'

Not always, he thought. Not the nights you spent in bed with me. Not the times you kissed me back.

He really had to stop thinking about her like this. And there was one sure-fire way of doing that. He'd prove to himself once and for all that he was not head over heels in love with anyone. Particularly with Kirsty.

Which was how he ended up taking Selina out for a Chinese meal. Selina, the liaison officer from the local college who'd wanted him to talk to her students…and who wanted a little more than that, too. Selina was elegant, beautiful, clever, good company—all the things he usually looked for in a girlfriend. And she was definitely interested in him. Interested enough to slip her shoe from her foot and slide her toes underneath the edge of his trousers as they drank white wine, waiting for their meal to arrive.

The old Ben would have smiled and capitulated. Flirted back. Played footsie under the table then taken her back to her place so they could get to know each other better. A lot better.

The new Ben wanted to run a mile. He was shocked to feel so embarrassed and out of place, and even more shocked to realise that this wasn't the foot he wanted caressing him. *That* foot belonged to someone else. Someone who was beautiful in a quiet, understated way. Someone whose mind worked faster than his own. Someone he was comfortable with. Someone...who was firmly off limits.

And he wasn't going to start thinking of her now.

He made an excuse about needing to use the men's room. It was as he made his temporary escape that he saw the group of hospital staff at the other end of the restaurant. A group that included Kirsty.

It was barely ten days since they'd last slept together, and he was already seeing someone else! The woman she'd seen him with in the hospital restaurant, with a smile as wide as the whole room. A smile that said Ben was all hers. And Kirsty knew from experience what was going to happen next.

No. She really couldn't bear this. She couldn't stay and watch him flirt with the woman. Especially when she could still remember what had happened in the linen cupboard, the last time she'd seen the woman with Ben. Something that would never, never happen again.

If he dared bring that woman back to their house, she'd kill him!

'Kirst, are you OK?' Jenny asked.

No, she wasn't. But Jenny had just given her the perfect excuse. 'Actually, I think I might be coming down with the lurgy that's doing the rounds,' Kirsty said. 'My head feels like someone's been using it for target practice.'

'I've got some paracetamol in my bag,' Nina offered.

'Thanks, but I think I'd be better off going home and having an early night.' Kirsty gave them a wan smile and fished in her purse for some money. 'Here. This is my share of the bill. Have a good time, and hopefully I'll see you tomorrow.'

'Let me call you a taxi,' Jenny said.

'The walk'll do me good.' And if she waited for a taxi, Ben would see her. She didn't particularly want to face him. Not until she'd got her best-friend-Kirst act firmly in place again. 'See you tomorrow.'

Before anyone else could protest—and, more importantly, before Ben came back from the loo—Kirsty had gone.

Ben stared at his reflection. 'It's not going to work, is it?' he asked the mirror. The moment he'd seen Kirsty, Selina had gone completely out of his mind. But what was he going to do about it? He'd already hurt Kirsty enough. Though the look that had just flashed over her face— before her eyes had shuttered and she'd turned away— told him he'd just made things a lot worse.

He couldn't—*couldn't*—give her the commitment she so clearly wanted.

The only way out of this mess would be to find her someone who could. Except he didn't know anyone who was good enough for her. A dating agency perhaps? Run a personal ad on her behalf and go through the replies himself? No, to both. He didn't want her fixed up with someone he didn't know, someone he couldn't trust never to hurt her.

You're being a dog in the manger, he warned himself. You don't want anyone to have her just because *you* can't have her.

Except he could have had her for ever. All he'd had to do was ask. And instead he'd thrown it all away.

Soberly, he walked back out to the restaurant and re-joined his date.

'Hi,' Selina purred.

He was about to say, Hi, yourself, when he remembered

who usually said that to him. He really, really shouldn't be here. 'Selina...I think we need to talk.'

'Oh?' Her blue eyes turned wary.

'It's not you. It's me,' he explained, feeling a complete and utter bastard as he saw the resignation flit over her face. 'Really. Anyone would be proud to go out with you—you're gorgeous and you're good company.' And now he sounded all oily and gushing, a complete sleaze-ball. 'The thing is, I've just split up with someone. I thought I was over it but...' He shrugged. 'I've realised it's too soon. Maybe if we'd met in a few months' time, things could have been different. I don't want to mess you about, so...can we just spend the evening together as friends?'

'Sure.' Selina's chin lifted.

It had to be hurt pride, Ben thought. She couldn't have fallen for him *that* quickly. Right now, he didn't like himself very much; he didn't see how anyone else could like him either.

He desperately wanted to talk to Kirsty—but how could he do it without making Selina feel as if he'd just dumped her for a better option? Maybe he could draw attention to the hospital crowd, say there was someone he needed to talk to about a case... Yes, that would do it.

'Sure. Go ahead,' she replied when he made the tentative suggestion. Her expression said she didn't believe a word of it.

Embarrassed and relieved at the same time, Ben headed over to Kirsty's table.

She wasn't there.

'I thought I recognised your voice,' he said to Jenny. But where was Kirsty? Loo, probably, he thought. He tried for lightness. 'Kirst not with you tonight?'

'No.'

No? But he'd seen her there only a few minutes before! And she'd seen him, he was sure of it.

'She's going down with the lurgy,' Nina said, 'but she wouldn't let us call her a taxi. You know Kirsty.'

'Stubborn as a mule,' he said wryly.

'We were, er, sorry to hear about the split, Ben,' Jenny said.

'It happens.'

'Though you're still friends?' Nina queried.

He nodded.

'Must be hard, sharing a house now,' Jenny commented.

That was one way of putting it. 'We manage.' He gave them a thin smile, knowing that he deserved the interrogation, and knowing that the group would all notice Selina within moments and draw their own conclusions. His ears would be burning for the rest of the evening, and deservedly so. 'See you later,' he said, and slunk back over to Selina.

Did Kirsty really have the lurgy? Or was it an excuse because she couldn't face seeing him with someone else? Guilt flooded through him and the meal he shared with Selina tasted like ashes. He felt even worse when he found himself asking his date to repeat her questions, time after time, because he simply wasn't paying attention. His thoughts kept drifting back to Kirsty and there was nothing he could do to stop them.

'Is everything all right? With your patient, I mean?' Selina asked.

Patient? What patient? Oh, yes. The one he'd invented so he could go over and talk to Kirsty. Except she hadn't been there. 'Yes, everything's fine, thanks.' Which was the biggest lie he'd told yet. This lying business was getting tricky—no wonder Kirsty was so dead set against it. 'I'm sorry. I…'

'Typical doctor. Mind on your work,' she said generously.

He agreed gratefully. 'I'm sorry this evening's been such a wash-out.' He didn't dare suggest trying to make up for it on another occasion. He had a nasty feeling that the next time would be even worse. 'I'll see you home,' he said quietly.

'That's OK. I'll get a taxi.'

'I'll ask them to order one when they bring our bill,' Ben said, signalling to the waitress.

He paid the bill, refusing to let Selina go halves with him. It was the least he could do, considering what a rotten evening he'd given her. If he'd met her before Scotland—before he'd fallen into bed with Kirsty—things might have been different. But right now his whole life was a mess, and he didn't have a clue how to get it back to the way it had been. The way he'd liked it, with Kirsty as his best mate and his love life on a more even keel.

When he'd seen Selina safely into the taxi, he thought about going home—then changed his mind. He had no idea what he was going to say to Kirsty and he didn't want to make things even worse between them. Instead, he headed for the beach and sat on the shingle at the edge of the sea with his knees bent and his arms wrapped round them. It was too early in spring for anyone else to be wandering along the beach at night, so he had just the stars and the sound of the waves swishing over the stones for company. The soft, regular murmur of the sea soothed him and he lost track of time as he sat there, occasionally throwing a flattish stone into the waves and watching it skim over the water's surface.

Eventually, the shingle started to dig into him. Time to head for home and face Kirsty. He still had no idea what to say to her, but somehow he'd find a way to make things all right. He *had* to.

There was no point in crying. It wasn't going to make Ben love her, was it? But Kirsty couldn't stop herself. Thinking of Ben in Selina's arms, sharing the pleasure he'd once given to *her*. That smile, the one that included only his lover and excluded the rest of the world. The look in his eyes. The sultriness in his voice.

Why did he have to be the one she'd fallen in love with? Why couldn't she have fallen for someone who'd actually let her into his life? Someone who wasn't terrified of even the word 'commitment'?

Why couldn't *she* have been the one he wanted, the love of his life?

She knew she was asking for the impossible: that Ben should love her back. But she couldn't help wanting it. Wanting him to hold her, wanting to feel the softness of his skin against hers, wanting to smell his clean, masculine scent. Wanting him to kiss her, make the whole world go away with his love-making. Wanting to be with Ben, secure in his bed and in the knowledge that he loved her as much as she loved him. But it was never going to happen.

Kirsty buried her face in the pillow, but it didn't stop the tears leaking out onto the cotton. And it didn't stop the ache in her heart.

The house was in complete darkness. If Kirsty really was coming down with the lurgy, she'd probably taken some paracetamol and gone straight to bed. If she wasn't…then he was the last person she'd want to see anyway. But he couldn't let this rest.

Hating himself for what he'd done to her, desperate to make things all right again, Ben went upstairs and knocked softly on her door. 'Kirst?'

She was hallucinating. The luminous hands on her clock said it was way too early for Ben to be home. Surely he should be with the lovely Selina, dancing the night away in a club before going back to her place?

Or… No. He wouldn't do that to her. He wouldn't have brought Selina back here with him…would he?

Kirsty ground her teeth and refused to answer.

To her horror, she heard the door handle turn, and light from the hallway filtered into her room as he opened the door.

Why couldn't he just leave her alone?

She tried to make her breathing sound deep and even. If he thought she was asleep he'd go away…wouldn't he?

Maybe Kirsty really did have the lurgy. She hadn't answered him, and Kirsty wasn't the sort to sulk. Whenever he'd upset her in the past, he'd known about it because she'd never minced her words. Things had changed between them lately, but surely *that* hadn't?

Part of him yearned to go over to her. As a doctor, he really ought to check her temperature—if she'd gone down with a fever she really needed tepid sponging and paracetamol. Ah, who was he trying to kid? He just wanted to be close to her. And he dared not. He couldn't offer her anything more than friendship and it wasn't fair to ask for more from her when he could give nothing in return.

Annoyed by his selfishness, he closed the door.

Kirsty could hardly breathe. Had he left her room—or was he about to walk over to her bed? She waited, her heart rate increasing with every second that passed. Then, as she realised that he'd left, a hollow feeling settled in her stomach. What was the old saying? Be careful what you wish for…

Well, that'd come true, all right. And it was her bad luck it hadn't been an earlier wish instead.

CHAPTER TWELVE

BEN was up early the next morning. If Kirsty was still feeling rough, she'd need something light for breakfast and he'd ring in sick for her. If she wasn't feeling rough...well, this would be the start of his apology. He made her some porage; while the cereal was thickening he squeezed a couple of oranges and poured the juice into a glass. He just resisted the impulse to add a flower to the tray—she'd probably throw it back in his face if he did that, and he acknowledged wryly that it was what he deserved—and carried it upstairs.

But Kirsty had clearly got up even earlier than he had, and quietly enough so as not to wake him. Because, when she didn't answer his tentative knock and he opened the door, balancing the tray on one arm, her curtains were open and her bed was neatly made.

Which meant that things between them were even worse than he thought.

Sighing, he took the tray downstairs again. He managed three mouthfuls of the porage before it choked him and he scraped the rest of the bowl into the bin. He gulped down the orange juice and washed up, vowing that he'd catch up with her at lunchtime and start to make things right then.

He didn't get the chance. A pile-up involving a chemical spill outside Southbay kept the A and E team rushed off their feet, while the queue of minor problems that usually came in during the day grew and grew. Ben ended up staying well past the end of his shift, with too many demands on his time to let him even think about Kirsty.

*   *   *

Kirsty, too, was busy, in Theatre. And stewing. She'd made another mistake this morning by asking Chambers a question. She and Paul had been discussing the merits of stapling and stitching over the last few days, and she'd raised the subject of whether stapling would be better than stitching in this case. The last thing she'd expected had been for Chambers to take it as a personal attack.

'As a consultant, Brown, I think I might have some idea of what I'm doing.'

'Of course. I wasn't questioning your abilities.'

The glare he'd shot her said he didn't believe it.

She subsided and continued assisting with the operation, even though she was itching to perform it herself. Why was he insisting on doing every case personally? Hadn't he worked with her and Paul for long enough now to know he could trust them to do their jobs and call him if they needed help?

'Close for me, Fisher,' Chambers directed.

Kirsty wanted to scream. Why wouldn't the man let her get on with her job? What was his problem? She couldn't think of anything she'd done to upset him—certainly nothing intentional—so why did they clash so badly? Was it her, or did he just hate all women? All women surgeons, she revised mentally.

He was staring at her. 'Is there a problem, Brown?'

You tell me. She stopped the words with an effort. 'I don't think so.'

'Then why are you glaring at me?'

Because you're stopping me doing the job I love and it's driving me crazy.

There was only one thing she could do. It was high risk and her working life could fall to pieces as a consequence—but, considering the mess the rest of her life was in, Kirsty didn't think things could get much worse. 'Could we have a word in your office when we've finished here, Mr Chambers?'

A brusque nod, and he swept off, leaving her to supervise Paul.

By the time Kirsty stood outside his office, she was having second thoughts. And third ones. Maybe head on wasn't the best way to deal with this…but, then again, she'd already tried being quiet and docile, and it just seemed to make him worse. Face a bully and he'll back down, she reminded herself. He'll back down.

She took a deep breath and rapped on the door.

'Come in.'

Feeling sick, she walked into Chambers's office and closed the door behind her.

'You wanted a word?'

She nodded. Get to the point, she told herself, digging her nails into her palms. 'Mr Chambers, I can't work like this.'

He smiled thinly. 'Not my problem, Brown.'

She lifted her chin. 'I'm a good surgeon, Mr Chambers. I just want to do my job.'

'That's what we all want.'

'There…seems to be a difficulty between us.'

He folded his arms and stared at her. 'Perhaps you should reconsider your attitude to my firm, Brown.'

But she wasn't the one with the attitude problem!

'Now, if there's nothing else?'

He wasn't even going to admit there was a problem—he'd as good as accused her of being paranoid and difficult to work with! Clearly he wasn't going to discuss it with her. And she certainly wasn't going to apologise for something she hadn't even done.

'No, nothing,' she said, and left his office.

She busied herself with paperwork, until Jenny rapped on the door of her office. 'Kirst, can I borrow you for a minute?'

'Sure. What's the problem?'

'We've been doing ten-minute obs on Maggie

Fletcher—' the patient she and Chambers had rowed over that morning '—and I don't like the look of her.'

'What's up?' Kirsty asked as she followed her friend over to the patient.

'Her BP's dropped, she's restless and a bit agitated, she looks pale and her skin's cold and clammy.'

'Pulse?' Kirsty asked, recognising the early signs of shock.

'Rapid and weak, and the pressure's dropping.'

'What about her dressing?'

Jenny shook her head. 'No external signs of haemorrhage.'

Which meant there could be internal loss of blood, leading to a fall in blood pressure and then shock—something that needed action. Fast. 'Where's Chambers?'

'On his break. That's why I asked you.'

Kirsty examined Maggie Fletcher courteously but swiftly, and came to the same conclusion as Jenny: the patient was losing blood and starting to go into shock. There were no external signs but clearly it was internal—caused by a slipped ligature, a shifting blood clot or maybe just increased blood pressure opening up veins that had collapsed previously. They had to get her into Theatre now, open her up and stop the haemorrhage before her circulatory system shut down.

'Better bleep him. I'll call the anaesthetics team.'

When Jenny had bleeped him for the second time with no answer, Kirsty decided to take matters into her own hands. 'Paul, it's you and me.'

'But—' the house officer began, clearly worried about operating without Chambers's permission.

'Paul, shock's serious. Circulatory failure means we could lose the patient. You know that as well as I do. We can't afford to wait, for Maggie Fletcher's sake. I'll take the rap, if I have to.'

As soon as she made the incision, Kirsty could see what the problem was: a slipped ligature. It didn't necessarily mean that Chambers had been negligent—sometimes they just happened. The important thing was to save the patient. She quickly repaired the damage, then Paul closed.

And it was when they got back to the ward that all hell broke loose.

'My office, Brown, *now*!'

She followed the consultant into his room and closed the door behind him.

'What do you think you were playing at?'

'Saving a patient's life.'

'*My* patient,' he reminded her.

'She was in classic early shock.'

'You should have bleeped me.'

'We did.' She folded her arms and stared at him. 'Twice.'

'Well, I didn't get the message. You should have tried again.'

'Shock's life-threatening. We didn't know where you were. What was I supposed to do—leave her until it was irreversible?'

'You should have—' Chambers began belligerently.

'Should have, schmould have!' Kirsty snapped back. 'When you're not around, the nursing staff come to me as the next most senior on the team. And I am *not* going to let patients die just to pander to your ego!'

'I beg your pardon?'

'You heard. I can't work with you. I've tried—God knows, I've tried—but everything I do is wrong in your eyes.'

'You're being over-emotional, Brown.'

Too damned right she was. Work was impossible and now that Ben had walked away from her, she had nothing left to lose. 'I've tried to talk to you about this…problem, whatever it is, between us before and you just won't listen. I save your patient and you take me to task; but if I'd left her to die, not daring to touch her because she's yours, I'd be breaking every moral code a doctor believes in and you'd be down on me like a ton of bricks.'

'Now you're being hysterical.' His lips thinned.

'Am I?' she flared back. 'You need to loosen up.'

'And you need to review your position in this firm,' he rapped back.

She shook her head. 'No need. I've had enough. I quit.' She slammed out of his office, ignoring the raised eyebrows and surprised looks from the rest of the ward staff.

She collected her things from her locker and stomped home, still fuming at Chambers's high-handed attitude. Then she slumped into a chair and stared at the wall, not really seeing anything. Which was how Ben found her, four hours later.

'Kirst, you left the door unlatched and—' He saw her face and was at her side in two strides. 'What's happened?'

'I don't have a job any more,' she replied tonelessly.

'*What?*'

'I said I don't have a job any more.'

'But why? What happened? Did you resign?'

'Yep.'

'But…' He froze. Surely she hadn't quit her job because of him? 'Why?'

'Because Chambers objected to me touching one of his patients.'

'Huh?'

She explained briefly.

'That's outrageous! It's constructive dismissal. Have you spoken to Personnel?'

'What's the point? What can they do about it?'

'Get you reinstated, that's what!'

'Ben, you don't get it, do you? Chambers hates me. If I go to Personnel and get reinstated, he'll make my life hell until I resign again—for good.'

'You're going to let him get away with it?'

She shrugged. 'What else can I do?'

'Fight him! Surely you're not going to let that—that low-life *scumbag* stop you doing what you really want, stop you being a top surgeon?'

'I was never going to make it anyway.'

'Yes, you were. You're good at your job, Kirst, and you're good with the patients.'

'Yes, but maybe I don't have the right temperament to deal with senior staff.'

'Oh, Kirsty.' He wanted to hold her, cuddle her pain away. In the old days, he wouldn't have even thought about it: he'd have given her the hug she needed. Now... Oh, why was he dithering like this? Sure, there was a lot they needed to resolve between them, but that could wait. Right now, Kirsty was hurting and he wanted to make it better.

He picked her up, sat on her chair and settled her on his lap with his arms tightly round her. 'Kirsty Brown, you're talking nonsense and you know it. You're one of the most popular doctors at the hospital.'

'That doesn't count.'

'Yes, it does.' His face hardened. 'Tomorrow morning, I'm going to be in Chambers's office, waiting for him. And when he gets in I'll—'

'Do nothing, Ben,' she cut in.

'What do you mean, do nothing? He's not getting away with this.'

'And you're not going to ruin your career over it. Fighting's a serious disciplinary offence. A sackable one.'

'I didn't say I was going to fight him, Kirst. I'm just going to talk to him. Though I admit I'd like to break every bone in his body right now.'

'Just leave it, Ben,' she said tiredly. 'It's not worth it.'

'Yes, it is.' *She* was worth it.

'Forget it, Ben. It's over.'

Ben's stomach turned to water. Over? What was she talking about? 'What's over?' he asked carefully.

'My job at Jimmy's. I could fight Chambers, yes—but

it'll get nasty. Really nasty. If I got my job back, it wouldn't be the same. I'd have divided the staff and there'd be an atmosphere. It wouldn't be fair on anyone.'

Relief and dismay coursed through him in equal measures. Dismay that she was giving up so easily—and relief that she hadn't been talking about them. 'So what are you planning to do?'

'Right now, I'm not sure. I'll have to get a reference from someone. Maybe I'll ask Tony.' She shook her head. 'No, that isn't fair. I don't want to worry him even more. I'll ask Viv in A and E. Then I'll do a locum job until I find something permanent.'

'Kirst, you really need to talk to Personnel about this. Maybe they could—I dunno, have a bit of a change-round, and swap you with one of the other surgical registrars.'

'There'd still be a lot of bad feeling, even if I didn't have to work with Chambers again. And what would happen when my consultant was on leave? I'd have to work under *him*, wouldn't I? I don't want to work like that, worrying about everything I do and say. I don't want to *live* like that, Ben.'

Ice slid down his spine. She wasn't talking just about work, was she? 'Kirsty, don't do anything rash.'

'I'm the sensible one, remember?'

The listlessness in her voice shocked him. 'Kirst, you—'

'Not now, Ben.'

Not now. The last time he'd said that to her, she'd been in his arms—and he'd kissed her. Right now, she was in his arms and he wanted to kiss her. But he knew that would be the worst thing he could do. He couldn't be her Dr Right, and although he could make her forget her troubles at work, it would be only temporarily.

Right now, he'd give her the support she needed. But when they'd cleared up all this mess about her job, maybe they could start working things out between them.

* * *

Kirsty wrote her official resignation letter the next morning. By the time Ben came back from a late duty, she'd organised a reference from Viv, the consultant in A and E. Five days later, she'd applied for half a dozen jobs, been interviewed twice and had found herself a locum position at Southampton, an hour's drive away.

'Kirst, all that extra travelling on top of your job—'

'Isn't important,' she cut in. 'I'm still working and I'm doing the job I trained for.'

'Miles away.'

She shrugged. 'I'll see how it goes. If the travelling's too much, I'll have to move nearer the hospital.'

She'd move. And then, for the first time in nearly ten years, Kirsty wouldn't be sharing a house with him. For the first time in nearly ten years, she wouldn't be there any more. His eyes widened. 'Kirst...'

'I'll manage,' she said. 'But I think we'll need to get a cleaner.'

'I'll do your share of the housework,' he said immediately.

'You barely do your own.'

He flinched. 'That'll change, I promise.'

She ignored him. 'I'll ring an agency tomorrow.'

Why should Kirsty have to find herself another job, just because her boss was such a prima donna? This really wasn't right, Ben thought angrily. He found it hard to be civil to Chambers when he had to refer cases up for surgery. He managed to keep things on a strictly professional level and gave the surgeon the information he needed about each case, even though he was itching to shake Chambers and ask him what the hell his problem was that he'd force out a brilliant registrar like that.

Maybe, Ben thought, that was the problem. Kirsty was brilliant. Maybe Chambers thought Kirsty would outshine him and had just decided to knock out the competition before anyone noticed. Maybe... It was just a hunch, but

Ben wanted to check it out. And he knew just the place to start: Personnel.

'I'm afraid I can't give you that sort of information, Dr Robertson,' Jan Kennedy said, looking worried.

He smiled. 'I promise I'm not going to cause problems for you. I don't want to see the file or anything like that. All I want to know is which hospital Mr Chambers came from.'

'Why don't you ask him?'

'It's…a delicate matter,' Ben said. Which was absolutely true, but also wasn't specific enough to get Kirsty into even more trouble.

The personnel officer thought about it. 'Well, I can't see what harm that'd do.' She glanced round at her colleagues, who all seemed busy, tapped quickly into the computer and looked up the information. 'City General in West London,' she said in a low voice.

'Thanks. I really appreciate it,' Ben said, smiling warmly at her. On his next break, he dropped into Personnel again. 'Just to say thanks,' he said, handing Jan a large box of chocolates.

'You didn't need to do that,' she protested, her cheeks becoming pink.

'Just to let you know I appreciate the trouble you went to,' Ben said. He smiled at her, and left the office.

A dozen phone calls later, plus a few very hefty favours owed, he had the information he wanted. And when Kirsty came home, tired out after a long day in Theatre plus an hour's travelling, he virtually dragged her into the kitchen.

'Ben, I'm not in the mood for any of your schemes,' she said. 'All I want is a bath and to fall into bed.'

Bed. Bad move to link Kirsty and bed in the same thought. He shook himself. 'No scheme. Sit down. Here.' He handed her a glass of freshly squeezed orange juice. 'Dinner will be…' he glanced at his watch '…three minutes after the kettle's boiled.'

'You don't have to cook for me,' she said, yawning and stretching. 'You've had a busy day yourself.'

'And I need to eat. It's just as quick to cook for two as it is for one.' His lips twitched. 'If you can call chucking fresh pasta into boiling water, heating up a jar of sauce and putting Parmesan on the top cooking.'

'That's all I was planning to do,' she admitted.

Ben was virtually hopping about from foot to foot, and he had the look on his face that usually heralded a new relationship. Kirsty's heart sank. Surely he wasn't expecting her to listen to him singing the praises of his latest love?

'All right. Out with it,' she said.

'What?'

'You're obviously dying to tell me something.'

'Chambers.'

She clenched her teeth. 'I don't care if I never hear that man's name again.'

'I found something out about him. He used to work at City General in West London.'

'So?'

'So, they had problems with him there—they virtually pushed him over to Southbay.'

'Ben, you don't know that for sure, and if you go round telling everyone that he'll probably sue you for libel.'

'Slander, actually, if it's verbal.'

Trust *him* to know the difference. 'Smug git,' she muttered.

'It's only slander if you can't prove it. And I can prove it, Kirst.'

She frowned. He could prove *what* exactly? 'Ben, what have you been doing?'

'Calling in a few favours.' He didn't admit to the ones he'd promised. 'Anyway, there's enough for you to build a case for constructive dismissal. He's done this kind of thing before—pushed and pushed and pushed until someone on his team resigned.'

'Why?'

'I didn't get quite that far in my research,' he confessed. 'But the thing is, he was known for having personality clashes with his juniors, particularly female ones. It got worse after his wife left him. Maybe you remind him of her or something.'

'I remind him of his ex-wife? Oh, thanks. You've just managed to put me off my dinner,' she said wryly.

Ben waved an impatient hand at her and dished up the pasta. 'Shut up and eat. Seriously, Kirst, you could have him for constructive dismissal. All you need is to ask Paul Fisher to give a witness statement.'

'And put his career on the line? I don't think so.'

'It won't come to that. All he has to do is tell the truth—that Chambers didn't treat you fairly. Jenny and Mandy on your ward will be witnesses, too.'

Kirsty glared at him. 'Ben, you're overstepping the mark.'

'I am not. I just had a little chat with them, that's all. They're as worried about you as I am.'

'You don't need to worry about me.'

'Kirst, you're wearing yourself out. Two hours' travelling on top of a heavy caseload isn't good for you. Or your patients.'

'I'm quite competent in Theatre, thank you very much!'

'I *know* that.' He rolled his eyes. 'I'm not trying to say you're useless. Just that you're doing too much. I don't want to see you wearing yourself out.'

'Ben, I'm fine.'

'Talk to Paul Fisher tomorrow,' he pleaded. 'Just talk to him.'

She sighed. 'If I get time.'

'Make time.'

'Stop fussing.'

'Promise me, and I'll shut up.'

Defeated, she nodded. 'OK. I'll talk to him.'

CHAPTER THIRTEEN

EXCEPT Paul didn't want to talk to her.

'Kirsty, I'm really sorry about what happened, but…I can't really do anything,' he said miserably. 'If he knew I was talking to you even now…' His voice tailed off.

She knew exactly what he meant. If Chambers found out that his SHO was talking to his ex-registrar and planning to help her with a constructive dismissal case, Paul would be out on his ear, too. Chambers would make the younger man's life hell until he resigned or became nervous enough to make a mistake that would justify Chambers dismissing him. 'You have to stand up against bullies,' she said gently.

'You did, and look what happened to you,' the younger doctor pointed out. 'I'm sorry—I know you helped me a lot when we worked together and I owe you, but I can't do this.'

'OK. No hard feelings. It wasn't very fair of me to ask,' Kirsty said. 'I'd better let you go before you get into trouble.' She put the phone down regretfully. She'd half expected Paul's reaction, but it still saddened her.

Ben was rather less charitable when he found out. 'Spineless little creep!' he said. 'I'll have a word with him tomorrow.'

'Leave it, Ben,' Kirsty said tiredly. 'He's got a point. If he leaves under a cloud—'

'Like you did?'

'I'm older, more experienced, and I can handle it. Drop it, Ben. Please?'

She could see by his face that he wanted to argue with her, but to her relief he nodded.

150

'I'm still going to build your case, Kirst.'

And what then? A row in court? What was the point? She'd already moved on. All she wanted now was to work as a surgeon—to do the job she loved and do it well. She couldn't do that in the same hospital as Guy Chambers. 'We'll see,' she said guardedly.

'I—I thought it was something I ate,' Marcia Hammond said, wincing as another wave of pain swept through her. 'Or maybe my appendix or something.'

'Where does it hurt?' he asked gently.

'My tummy,' she said, touching her abdomen lightly and then pulling her fingers away with a wince. 'It hurts.'

'Have you missed a period at all?' Ben asked.

She shrugged. 'Don't know. I'm not that regular—anything between four and six weeks.'

'Can you remember when your last period was?' he asked.

'Five, six weeks ago?'

'I'm sorry to ask you such a personal question, but is there any possibility you might be pregnant?'

'Hardly. I haven't got a boyfriend.'

He decided not to press her, but then she began to gag. Recognising the signs, Ben ducked out of the cubicle and grabbed a bowl from the nearest trolley. 'Here,' he said, and she promptly vomited into it.

Not green, he noted as he mopped her face and glanced into the bowl, so possibly not her appendix.

'It hurts,' she said, her face paling.

Ben noted the sweating, and quickly checked her pulse. Rapid and weak, and her hands were cold. A quick check of her blood pressure showed it was dropping.

'Marcia, I need to examine you. I'll try to be gentle,' he said, 'but just tell me if it hurts too much and I'll stop.'

Her abdomen was distended and tight; she flinched as he touched her. Textbook presentation, he thought, but she was adamant that she couldn't be pregnant. She was clearly too tender for him to give her a pelvic examination, but he needed to be sure—an acute ruptured tubal pregnancy was as life-threatening as a ruptured appendix. 'Marcia, I'd like to do an ultrasound just to check something out. And…I know you say you can't be pregnant, but I'm going to do a pregnancy test.'

'But…' Her eyes widened. 'Oh, hell.'

'What?'

'I… It was about three, four weeks ago. I had a night out with the girls, met a bloke, drank too much—and I can't remember the rest of the evening. I woke up in my own bed so he must have dropped me back at my place.' She closed her eyes. 'Oh, God. I can't even remember doing it with him.'

'Don't beat yourself up. It happens,' Ben said sympathetically.

'But I never get that drunk. I…I felt ill all the next day, but I thought it was a hangover. Maybe…'

Rohypnol, the 'date-rape' drug? Maybe, but they didn't have time to think about that now. Not if he was right. 'We'll talk about that later, but I really need to check you out right now,' he said gently.

The ultrasound and the pregnancy test confirmed his suspicions. 'I'm sorry, Marcia. You're having an ectopic pregnancy—that means the egg implanted in your Fallopian tube instead of in your womb, and as it's grown it's stretched the tube and caused it to burst.' He squeezed her hand. 'I'm so sorry. We'll need to operate to remove the foetus and the tube.'

She stared at him in horror. 'But I'm only twenty-two! You can't remove my tubes! What if I want to get married and have kids in a few years' time?'

'It doesn't mean you can't ever have children,' Ben said, 'but you will only have one Fallopian tube so that may make things harder for you to get pregnant in the future. The gynae team will be able to give you some good advice and more information, but my main priority right now's to stop your pain.'

'But…' She began to sob. 'This can't be happening.'

'I'm sorry.' He squeezed her hand. 'We'll get you up to Theatre. Is there anyone you'd like us to call?'

'My mum.' She covered her face with her hands, her voice broken as she muttered, 'I want my mum.'

'We'll get her for you. Just tell me her number,' Ben said, 'and she'll be here by the time you're back out of Theatre.'

Poor kid, he thought as he left the cubicle, giving Marcia's mother's number to the A and E receptionist before he rang the obs and gynae team. Thank heavens it wasn't Kirsty's old team he had to ring. Chambers was the last person Marcia needed right now—she needed someone thoughtful and kind, who'd talk her through the op and explain her options afterwards, listen to her and help get to the bottom of her 'missing' evening. Someone like Kirst—

He stopped himself. Job first, he reminded himself, and rang up to the obs and gynae team.

At the end of another week, Kirsty had to admit to herself that she was tired. Bone-achingly weary. The travelling on top of a demanding job really was getting too much for her. Maybe she should get digs in Southampton and just come back to Southbay on her days off. Maybe she should move to Southampton, full stop, until she found a permanent post. She was still thinking through her options when she came home to an empty house and found her post stacked neatly on the table. Including a brown envelope offering her a registrar's post in a teaching hospital in London.

It was a chance to work in a department with a cutting-edge reputation in keyhole surgery, the area she wanted to work in. A fresh start, where her row with Chambers wouldn't be hanging over her. And when she'd passed her last set of exams she'd be made up to senior reg with research duties, with the prospect of a consultancy in a reasonably short space of time. She'd be mad to turn it down. But it was also a good two and a half hours from Southbay, too far to commute. And that meant leaving Ben.

She was just about to start listing all the reasons—other than Ben—to stay in Southbay when the phone rang.

'Hello?'

'Is Ben there?' a breathy, feminine voice asked.

Kirsty didn't recognise the voice, which made it a fair bet that the woman wasn't a colleague. So did that mean Ben was back to his old ways, having a new girlfriend every three weeks? Clearly the blonde college liaison officer hadn't lasted long either. 'I'm afraid not,' she said coolly. 'Can I take a message?'

'Tell him that Becca rang. He knows the number,' the voice cooed.

Kirsty just bet he did! 'I'll leave him a note.'

'Thanks, sweetie. *Ciao!*'

Kirsty was actually growling as she put the phone down, though half a packet of chocolate biscuits and two lattes later she decided that Becca, whoever she was, had actually done her a favour. She'd finally woken Kirsty up to the fact that what had happened between her and Ben had been just sex. Mind-blowing sex, admittedly, but just sex. If Kirsty stayed in Southbay, she'd have to live with that—and grin and bear it every time Ben went out with one of his drop-dead-gorgeous women.

Could she do that?

In the old days, yes. Now… Despite all her protests to the contrary, she couldn't go back to thinking of Ben as just her best mate. She couldn't forget what they'd shared. And she couldn't forget that she loved him.

It was time, Kirsty thought, to make a clean break. Forcing back the tears—pointless tears, because they wouldn't make Ben love her back—she scribbled Ben a note, left it under the salt-cellar, then switched on her computer and typed out her acceptance letter for the London job.

It was three days before she saw Ben to tell him the news—she'd wanted to tell him face to face rather than leaving him a note, but he'd been out when she'd come home late, or working late when she'd been home early and she'd ended up going to bed before he'd come in.

'What do you mean, find myself a new flatmate?'

'I've been offered a job in London. It's a dream job, Ben. I'd be mad to turn it down. It's in a teaching hospital, doing keyhole surgery, a post with research duties attached when I've finished my exams. Everything I've always wanted.'

'I see.' His face was unreadable. 'When did this happen—today?'

'Three days ago,' she admitted.

'Three days ago,' he echoed.

'Look, if you'd been here I'd have discussed it with you,' she said, catching the quickly masked flicker of hurt in his eyes. 'You were out. I had to make a quick decision. So I listed the pros and cons and decided it was the right thing to do.' The main pro being that she wouldn't have to pretend to Ben that she thought of him just as her friend.

'So you're going to drop the case against Chambers?'

'I never wanted to make the case in the first place,' she reminded him quietly.

'Right.'

Why did she feel so guilty? *She* wasn't the one who'd called a halt to their relationship. And she really, really couldn't stay here, watching him date other women and longing for what they had. But that look on his face... She'd hurt him by not even discussing it with him. 'We'll still be friends. It'll just be long distance, that's all.' For the first time since she'd known him. 'We can arrange our off-duty so I can come down and paddle in the sea with you, and you can come up for the odd weekend in London. We can go and feed the flamingoes in Hyde Park and what have you. Have a picnic at Kew. Do the Planetarium,' she offered. The kind of things they'd enjoyed doing together as students in London.

'Of course.' But his smile, to Kirsty, looked forced.

The night before Kirsty left, Ben organised a surprise party for her. Everyone from A and E and the surgical ward was there, apart from Chambers. Paul Fisher looked slightly sheepish but gave her a hug and told her not to forget them. She was touched when Jenny presented her with a beautiful framed watercolour of the beach at Southbay, painted by a local artist, on behalf of all her friends at the hospital.

She absolutely refused to dance, though, with Ben or with anyone else. Ben had no shortage of willing partners, and Kirsty knew she'd made the right decision to leave. Even seeing him dancing with women she knew were just colleagues made her stomach knot with jealousy. Funny to think it had only been a few weeks ago when they'd danced together at their impromptu engagement party.

The walk home was a nightmare. They both avoided the subject, but they both knew the other was thinking of the previous party, the party where they'd finally fallen into each other's arms. Right now, it would be so easy to turn to each other, hold each other and...

No. Ben was off limits, Kirsty reminded herself.

'See you in the morning,' Kirsty said as soon as they were back at their house. 'It's going to be a long day tomorrow—I need my sleep.'

''Night, Kirst,' Ben said quietly. She was aware of him watching her all the way up the stairs, but dismissed it as an idle fancy.

She slept badly, and there were dark circles under her eyes the next morning as she made coffee and munched her toast in between loading boxes into the Transit van Ben had hired. She didn't dare look at Ben for long enough to see whether he had matching circles under his eyes. The drive to London was awkward. Ben kept fiddling with the radio station rather than talk to her, and Kirsty was relieved at not having to be polite.

'You really didn't have to do this, you know,' she said as he walked in the door of her first-floor flat with the last of the boxes.

'Of course I did. Any mate worth their salt would check out your neighbours and make sure your new place isn't damp or falling to pieces.'

'I did view the place twice before I rented it,' she reminded him.

'Yeah. Where do you want these shelves, then?' he asked.

She showed him, and made them both a coffee while he drilled and hammered and did the kind of DIY stuff she hated. He barely paused to drink his coffee, so she unpacked while he finished putting up her pictures and shelves.

'Pizza or Chinese?' she asked when the noise stopped.

Ben glanced at his watch. 'Actually, I'd better be getting back. I'm on early tomorrow. I'll grab something on the way home.'

Home. She stifled the surge of longing. Southbay wasn't *her* home any more.

'Right. Well, thanks for all your help.'

'Pleasure.'

Was this how it ended? Polite strangers? Awkwardly, she hugged him. 'Take care of yourself.'

'You, too. I'll ring you tomorrow to see how your first day went.'

'Right.'

She watched him from the window. He glanced up as he reached the van and put his hand up in salute. And then he was gone and her flat seemed dark and gloomy, and Kirsty found herself mooching round.

This is crazy, she thought. We both knew it was time to move on.

But she hadn't expected it to hurt so much.

The house felt empty. Kirsty hadn't taken that much with her, but there were pale squares on the wall where some of her prints had hung, and Ben noticed the spaces on the mug-tree where Kirsty's mugs had hung. He noticed the gaps on the shelves where her books had been, the gaps in the CD rack. It felt as if half his life had just disappeared.

The sooner he found a new housemate, the better. He should have started looking as soon as she'd told him she was leaving, but he hadn't wanted to try and replace her before she'd even gone.

Though maybe Kirsty wasn't replaceable.

He stifled the thought. Her career was important to her. She would have been crazy to turn down the London job. It was the opportunity of a lifetime.

But a small part of him still wished she *had* turned it down.

'Grow up, Robertson,' he told himself loudly. 'Time to move on.' Just like Kirsty had.

Though he found himself rushing home the next day and dialling her number. Funny, he hadn't even had to look it up. He shook himself. No, it didn't mean anything. He'd always had a retentive memory.

The phone rang. And rang. 'C'mon, c'mon, pick up!' he said impatiently.

'This is Kirsty Brown. I can't come to the phone right now. Leave a message after the beep and I'll call you back.'

His throat dried. He didn't want to talk to her answering machine. He wanted to talk to *her*, find out all about her first day.

He tried again, half an hour later.

And half an hour after that.

And half an hour after *that*.

Finally, as he was forking over the scrambled eggs he'd made himself and had then decided he didn't really fancy after all, the phone rang.

'Hello?'

'Do you understand what answering machines are for, Benjamin Robertson?' a tart voice asked him.

He grinned. 'Yes. But they don't have conversations with you, Kirsty Brown.'

'Hmm. Just as well I dialled 1471, isn't it?'

Well, who else would have called her? Her parents, he supposed, and her brothers. Maybe even Morag, who hadn't made a single comment about Kirsty choosing to go to London. She'd just said, 'Hmm,' in that way grandmothers had.

'So how was your first day, then?' he asked.

'Brilliant,' she enthused. 'Ben, the stuff they're doing here—it's light years away from Southbay. I've got more laparoscope work booked for the next week than I've done in the months since Tony went off sick. And Ted's brilliant.'

'Ted?' That tight feeling in his stomach wasn't jealousy. Of course it wasn't.

'Ted Baker. My consultant. He really knows what he's doing and he's an excellent teacher. He's very much like Tony, actually—a younger version.'

'Younger?' The word was out before he could stop it.

'He's thirty-seven.'

Ben only just managed to stop himself asking if this Ted was single, too. 'That's good,' he said carefully. 'A team with a young outlook.' Young, gifted and it sounded as if Kirsty adored him already. Ben wondered if warts could appear all over someone's nose just from wishing.

'The scrub team's great, too. And the ward staff—

though I think we'd have to go a long way to find someone like Jenny.'

And an even longer way for him to find someone like
Kirsty. 'Mmm.'

Kirsty chattered on excitedly about the operations she'd
performed that day, and how Ted had glued a damaged
spleen rather than removing it. Although it was good to
hear her so enthusiastic again, hear the pleasure in her job
that Chambers had nearly suffocated, Ben couldn't help
feeling…excluded. He had only a very part-time part in
her new life, and it hurt.

Stop it, he told himself. This is Kirst's chance to shine
and you're not going to spoil it for her.

'So how's everything with you?'

'You know. Same as always.'

'Any replies to your ad yet?'

'Not yet.' Because he hadn't placed it. Having someone
else to fill the house was a good idea, he knew. Right now
the place seemed empty. At the same time, he couldn't
stand the thought of anyone in Kirsty's place.

'I'm sure you will soon.'

She chattered on for another quarter of an hour. 'I'd
better let you go,' she said.

'Yeah. Kirst, your flat's near the hospital, isn't it?'

'Walking distance,' she confirmed.

'They work later shifts than we do, then?'

'No. I went for a drink with Ted after work. Ted and
the team,' she amended.

Serious, studious Kirsty had gone for a drink after
work? But *he'd* virtually had to drag her away from her
books! Then he realised what she'd said. She'd gone out
with *Ted*. Her first day away from him, and she'd already
gone out on a date with another man…

Ben shook himself. It was none of his business anyway.
He'd had his chance with her and he'd blown it. He
should be nice and wish her luck. Wish her the happiness
she deserved. He shouldn't be wanting to rip this Ted—

a man he'd never even met—limb from limb. 'I'll ring you later in the week, then.'

'Cheers. Give my love to everyone.'

'Will do.' Ben's heart was heavy when he replaced the receiver.

Things didn't get any better over the next few weeks. Ben discovered that he couldn't even flirt with his patients any more the Saturday afternoon he had to do a reduction on a dislocated shoulder.

'Dirty tackle,' the shapely brunette captain of Southbay Ladies FC told him cheerfully. 'The cow owes me an Indian *and* a few pints tonight.'

Ben didn't even notice how good her figure was in the well-cut shorts and baggy top. He was too busy looking at the anterior dislocation. 'Don't tell me—you took a tumble, stretched your hand out and landed on top of it?'

'That's about right, Doc,' she agreed.

The body had rotated over the hand and caused the anterior dislocation. It was common in this age group, Ben remembered, usually through a sporting accident or being thrown from a motorcycle. 'We'll get you to Radiography just to check,' he said, 'but we'll make it fast—the longer it's out, the harder it is to fix.'

Radiography confirmed his diagnosis and he smiled at the footballer. 'The good news is, it's easy to fix—it might hurt a bit, though, so I'll give you something to relax your muscles and something to ease the pain.'

She lifted her eyebrows suggestively. 'I'm all yours, Doc.'

For a moment, Ben almost told her that he was married. Or gay. Anything to stop the way her lips curved like that—because the sexy, inviting smile he wanted belonged to someone more petite, someone with eyes that turned gold. He shook himself, then gave her an opioid analgesic and IV diazepam. When he'd trained, they'd placed patients like this prone on a trolley with their arm hanging over the side: the combination of gravity and the muscle relaxant usually led to the shoulder going back in naturally. He had a feeling that this one would need a bit more help so he manipulated her shoulder, easing the bone back to where it should be.

Within minutes, the footballer was sitting normally again and giving him a real come-hither smile.

'Take it easy for the next few days. You'll need a body bandage,' he said, 'including to your forearm—just to make sure your shoulder doesn't slip out again. The more it happens, the more likely it is you'll need surgery. You'll need some physio as it is.'

'Gonna do it for me, Doc?'

How easy it would be to say yes. Except he didn't want to. He wanted *Kirsty*.

'No. There is something I want to test, though.' Sometimes a dislocated shoulder could affect the nerves running under the armpits, leaving the patient unable to use the arm properly and needing months of physio. He needed to check for any signs of axillary nerve palsy, as it was called, so he took a needle. 'Just tell me if you feel this,' he said, lightly pricking the outer aspect of her shoulder.

'Ouch!'

He smiled. 'You'll do. Good luck with the rest of the warm-up matches.'

'Yeah. Last time *I* play a friendly with that daft cow's team,' she said wryly. 'You want a ticket to a match next season, you just ring the team and ask for me. Lorraine Dexter.' The look in her eyes made it clear she was offering more than just a ticket.

'Thanks. I will,' Ben said, though he knew he had no intention of ringing.

Although he didn't actually advertise for a new flatmate, the hospital grapevine was working well and Ben had several offers—offers which he turned down with increasingly feeble excuses. It just wouldn't feel right, having someone in Kirsty's room.

He tried going out for a meal or to the cinema, but he knew he was less than good company and the girls he asked out didn't seem to mind when he didn't suggest a second date. In the end, he stopped going out altogether. Nothing in his world seemed to fit any more. Whenever he phoned Kirsty she was out, and whenever she phoned him back she was full of Ted this and Ted that.

It was unbearable.

Part of him wanted to storm down to London and check out the fabulous Ted Baker for himself. Was the hotshot consultant really everything Kirsty seemed to think he was? Was he treating Kirsty properly, and not messing her about? And anyway, wasn't it unethical to get involved with someone on your team?

'Listen to yourself. Anyone'd think you're jealous,' he told his reflection scornfully.

He didn't have the right to be jealous. Hadn't he pushed Kirsty away when she'd told him she loved him? She owed him absolutely nothing. She was a free agent. She could go out with anyone she pleased—she could be dating *twenty* big-shot consultants if she wanted, and it was none of his business.

'Get a grip, Robertson,' he said roughly. 'She's not yours.'

She had been, once.

But she'd left him.

And he'd finally lost his 'Dr Charming' tag. He'd overheard the senior sister on A and E describing him as 'Dr Grouchy' to the new house officer when she was showing the doctor round the department. He hadn't stayed to hear the rest.

When life was falling apart, there was only one place Ben could go. He swapped some shifts round to give him a break of four days, rang his grandmother and flew to Inverness.

'You look terrible' was the first thing she said to him when he'd parked his hire car outside her cottage.

'Gran…' For the first time since he was fourteen, Ben leaned his head on her shoulder and hid his face from the world. Letting her enfold him in her arms. He hadn't cried since he was a child, but this felt as bad as all the times his mother had abandoned him. He literally shook with the effort of controlling himself but, even so, a single tear forced its way through his eyelid, searing his skin. This wasn't fair to his grandmother. He was supposed to be the strong one now. He clenched his fists, willing himself to be strong, then finally lifted his head.

'Sorry about that, Gran,' he said, forcing a smile to his face.

'It's been a long time coming, love.' She stroked his face. 'Ready to talk about it?'

'Yes—no—I don't know,' he said miserably.

'Then let me guess. It's Kirsty, isn't it?'

He nodded. 'But it's too late, Gran.'

'I love you,' Morag said softly to her grandson. 'I'm proud of you. But, for such a bright lad with so many qualifications, you can be *incredibly* thick.'

'Thick?' He stared at her in amazement. 'What do you mean?'

'You love her, don't you?'

Ben spread his hands. 'I don't know what love is.'

'Yes, you do. But you're afraid of it.'

His chin came up. 'I'm not afraid.'

Morag didn't contradict him in so many words, but she took his hands and squeezed them. 'Not everyone's like your mother. I'm not. Kirsty's not. *You're* not.'

'Aren't I?' he asked wryly. 'I pushed her away, Gran.'

'Hmm. So that's why you call her four or five times a week to see how she's getting on, is it?'

He flushed. 'How do you know about that?'

'Because she rings me once a week.'

'She's found someone else. Ted. Her consultant,' he added bitterly.

Morag smiled. 'You think so?'

'She's always going out with him.'

'And the rest of the team. They're a friendly bunch.'

'We're friendly at Southbay. She didn't go out with us very often.'

'Ben, listen to yourself. You're jealous.'

'As hell,' he admitted. 'But it's too late.'

'Why don't you just go and see Kirsty, tell her what she means to you?'

'I can't.'

'Why not?'

'Because she left me, Gran. She doesn't want me. She walked away.'

'How do you know she doesn't want you, Ben?'

'I just do.'

The silence stretched out between them for a long, long while; Ben stared at the surface of the scrubbed pine table until he couldn't even see it any more. Eventually, he lifted his head and met his grandmother's enquiring gaze. 'If I tell her... Supposing she rejects me, Gran?' Just the way his mother had, always promising her love for him and always backing away. Late birthdays, late Christmases, always the afterthought. Always waiting for the proud smile of a mother meeting him in the primary school playground, the protective cuddle when he woke from a nightmare, the hugs and kisses that never came. Would it be like that with Kirsty, when she realised that he was basically unlovable? Had she realised that already and that was why she'd gone away?

'Supposing she *doesn't* reject you?' Again, Morag squeezed his hands. 'Sometimes, Ben, you have to take a risk. Right now, you're hurting. You love her—but you're too scared to let her love you. What's the worst thing that could happen?'

He closed his eyes. Wasn't it obvious? The same thing that had happened with his mother, over and over and over again. 'She'll leave.'

'She already has. And you've survived,' Morag pointed out. 'What's the best thing that could happen?'

That she'd hold him. Love him. Keep his heart safe. Wrap it in white lace and promises—promises she'd keep. Marry him. Live with him and be his love. Be the first thing he saw when he opened his eyes, the last thing he saw before he fell asleep.

Though he couldn't bring himself to voice his hopes. Didn't they say if you wished aloud it'd never come true?

'Think about it,' Morag said softly. 'Go for a walk and think about it.'

He did. He sat down in the wood, where he'd taken Kirsty to see the bluebells all those weeks before, and he thought about it. All his no-commitment relationships— they hadn't been real. Just glitz and glamour, fun and bright lights. Exactly the way he'd planned them, with no chance of getting hurt on either side.

The only real 'commitment' relationship had been with Kirsty. She'd always been there for him—like the time he'd thought he was going to fail a paper at the end of their first year and she'd made him study with her, had pretended that she'd needed help with the subject when she'd really been the one to help him. And when they'd shared a house, it had been a home. A proper home. Not just a place to stay, like the house was now. It had been home because Kirsty had been there.

All the time he'd thought his feelings for Kirsty had been platonic. Then he'd discovered there had been lust, too. And lust plus friendship equalled...

He sighed heavily. He'd left it too late. He'd pushed her away. What right did he have to ask her to take a chance on him? Look at his track record. One girlfriend after another, a bit of fun. Kirsty deserved more than that.

He wanted to give her more than that.

But how?

He didn't know where to start. How to start.

Supposing she laughed at him? No, Kirsty wasn't like that. If she rejected him, she'd be kind about it. But it would still be rejection. Supposing the way she felt about him had changed—supposing she'd grown tired of waiting for him to realise what was so blindingly obvious to everyone else, and she was over him? Supposing she'd met someone else—someone who'd paid her the attention she deserved?

The only way he could find out was to put his heart on the line and ask her. He couldn't do that. But what was the alternative? Spending every empty day without her, trying to fill the seconds, the minutes, the hours, the years, and knowing that he'd thrown away the best thing that had ever happened to him. He couldn't do that either.

What now? he asked himself.

The only thing he could think of was to start in the middle and muddle his way through. Take a chance—and trust her.

CHAPTER FOURTEEN

COLD, wet and decidedly grumpy. If someone had asked Ben to describe himself in five words, they'd have fitted perfectly. Why on earth couldn't Kirsty have rented a flat with a porch so unexpected visitors could shelter from the fine London drizzle that soaked through clothes in seconds? Even more pertinently, why couldn't she come home on time?

Probably because she was out with Ted bloody Baker, he answered himself.

Well, he was here now. And he was staying put until he'd talked to her.

He saw her before she saw him. Running down the street, sharing a huge golfing umbrella with a man. Laughing with him. The bloke even had his arm possessively round Kirsty's shoulders—round *his* Kirsty's shoulders!

Leave. Leave now, a voice in his head whispered.

Stubbornly, he stayed put. He wasn't going until he'd talked to Kirsty. They needed to sort this out once and for all.

The gate creaked open, and Kirsty walked down the red-and-black chequered path. And stopped dead at the sight of the man sitting on her doorstep. 'Ben,' she breathed.

'Hello, Kirst,' he said, unsmiling.

'Ben—I wasn't expecting you.'

'I know.'

'Ted, this is Ben Robertson—Ben, this is Ted Baker, my consultant.'

Ben looked at the surgeon. Tall, dark-haired, blue-eyed, handsome—and he looked slightly concerned. Worried

168

that Ben was about to snatch his lady-love? Well. That choice was Kirsty's. Ben just hoped that she made the right one. He stood up, and noted that Ted was almost exactly his own height. He held his hand out stiffly. 'Hello.'

'Good to meet you, Ben.'

Ben only just resisted the urge to squeeze the man's hand as hard as he could. But Kirsty deserved better. He wasn't going to be childish about it.

'Kirsty's told me a lot about you,' Ted continued.

'And you.' He had to face it, Ted was all she ever talked about nowadays. He forced himself to be polite. 'I hear you're an expert with glue.'

'I try,' Ted said with a smile.

Hell. He might have known that the man would be *nice*. Kirsty wouldn't pick a bad 'un. Apart from himself, that was.

'You're soaked,' Kirsty said accusingly.

'It's raining,' Ben deadpanned back.

'If you'd told me you were coming, I'd have been here to meet you.'

'Uh-huh.'

They stared at each other for a long, long moment.

'I'll, um, leave you to it,' Ted said.

Kirsty nodded. 'Thanks for seeing me home safely, Ted. See you tomorrow.'

'See you. Nice to have met you, Ben,' Ted added, and walked away.

Kirsty opened the door in silence, and Ben closed it behind him before following her up the stairs.

'You'd better get out of those wet clothes,' she said.

'I don't have any dry ones.'

'Have a shower and wrap yourself in a towel. I'll stick your clothes in the tumble-drier.'

Ben nodded and did as he was told.

Stupid, stupid, *stupid*, he told himself as he stripped off in her tiny bathroom and stepped into the shower. You should have phoned her first. Or walked away. Ted obviously cares for her. He saw her home safely; he'll look after her properly. He was probably expecting to come in for coffee, a glass of wine, end up in Kirsty's bed...

Kirsty's bed was definitely not the right subject to think about. He turned the shower to cold until he was back under control, then dried off and wrapped the towel loosely around his waist. He padded back to the kitchen with his wet clothes in a bundle under his arm.

Kirsty's mouth went dry as she turned round and saw Ben standing there, his skin still damp from his shower and his hair wet. He looked positively edible. She could still remember the time he'd made love to her in the shower, and the thought sent tiny needles of desire zinging through her body.

'Do you want a coffee?' she asked shakily.

'If you're making one, yes, please.'

'OK.' She turned her back to him; by the time she'd made two coffees and put them on the small round kitchen table she was back in control. 'I'll put these in the drier,' she said, taking Ben's soggy clothes.

He nodded his thanks and sat down at the table. Kirsty fiddled with the drier for as long as she dared and then joined him at the table.

'So. What brings you here?' she asked, her voice overbright.

'I wanted to see you.'

She frowned. 'Ben, are you all right?'

'Why?'

'You look...' Her voice faded. He looked terrible. He'd lost weight and there was a severity in his face she'd never seen before. 'Is Morag all right?' she asked, suddenly making the connection.

'She's fine. I've just come from Scotland, actually.' He should have been back in Southbay, but he'd begged enough favours to give him a day or two's grace.

'Ben…what's wrong?'

'You,' he told her.

'Me?'

He nodded slowly. 'It's hard for me to say this—especially when you're fully dressed and I'm only wearing your towel, and you could throw me out at any time, and—'

She leaned across and took his hand. 'And you're waffling, Benjamin Robertson.'

'Yeah,' he admitted ruefully. 'Kirst…I don't know where to start.'

'Try the beginning.'

'I don't know where the beginning is.'

'Try the middle,' she suggested.

Exactly what he'd told himself. 'OK.' He took a deep breath. 'Are you in love with Ted Baker?'

'Ted?' To his horror, she actually laughed.

'What's so funny?'

'Ted,' she told him, trying desperately to keep a straight face, 'is my friend. He's off limits.'

Ben had been her friend once. And *he'd* been off limits. Until he'd dragged her into that ridiculous engagement. He went cold. Supposing… 'Because he's your boss?' he asked carefully.

'Because he's in a relationship. A very long-standing relationship.'

'He's *married*? You're in love with a married man?'

She shook her head and her eyes crinkled at the corners with amusement. 'Ted's gay.'

He narrowed his eyes. 'Does Gran know this?'

'I might have told her—I can't remember. Why?'

'Doesn't matter.' He stared at her. 'Are you in love with him?'

'No, I'm not.' She pursed her lips. 'Ben, I've come home to find you sitting on my doorstep, soaked through. Don't I deserve an explanation?'

'I'm trying,' he growled. 'I just… Look, I find…

relationships difficult.' If he was going to tell her the truth, he knew it ought to be the whole truth. 'Gran thinks it's because of my mother,' he admitted.

'Your mother?' Kirsty said softly.

She was still holding his hand. He tightened his grip. 'Sarah,' he clarified. 'She didn't do commitment either.'

'Just because you're her son, it doesn't mean you're like her,' Kirsty pointed out.

'Doesn't it? Every time anyone gets close to me, I back off. I keep everyone at arm's length. I make it clear all my relationships are no-strings, just for fun, so everyone knows where they stand right from the start and no one gets hurt. Except…' he paused for a long while '…you. And then I pushed you away.'

When she'd told him she loved him. She swallowed hard. 'Yes.'

'Kirst, I know this is probably way too late, but…' He sighed. 'Oh, hell, I'm making a mess of this. Anyway, I asked you to be my fiancée because I thought you were safe—because you didn't do relationships either.' He stared at her. 'I asked you why, once, and you said it was because of your career.'

She flushed. 'It is.'

'Really?' He tipped his head on one side. 'I've been thinking about it and there's something that doesn't add up. You've got a real thing about lies. I mean, more than just the usual sense of right and wrong. And the bullying you told Adam about—it wasn't just Chambers, was it?'

'Drop it, Ben,' she warned.

'Kirst, there've been too many secrets between us already.'

She closed her eyes. 'This isn't about me.'

'Yes, it is. You and me. *Us.* Tell me, Kirst,' he said softly. 'Who hurt you so badly?'

She couldn't speak. Smothering an oath, he pulled her onto his lap. 'Tell me, Kirst.'

With his arms wrapped round her like that, she could barely think straight.

'I don't do relationships because I don't know how. Why do you avoid them?'

'Because of Luke,' she forced out eventually.

'Luke?'

'Don't you remember him? In our first year. A bit like you—he had women swooning over him all over the place.'

He ignored the bitterness in her voice and stroked her hair. 'What happened?'

'He asked me out. One of the major heartthrobs in our year asked me out—plain, studious little Kirsty Brown. I thought he liked me. I thought…and then I heard them,' she choked out. 'Luke and his friends. There was a book running. They were betting on how quickly he could add me as a notch to his bedpost. The girls as well—how could anyone as dumpy and plain as me think I could attract someone as stunning as Luke? All the time I thought he wanted me, that he cared, he was doing it for a bet. Money.' She lifted her head. 'I heard him cashing it in. They were all *laughing* at me, Ben, because I'd let him make love to me and I'd been stupid enough to think it was because he wanted me.'

'And all of them were kicked out at the end of the first year for failing their exams. Doesn't that tell you something?'

She shrugged. 'They partied too hard.'

'No. They didn't have what it takes to be good doctors—the decency, the brains, the sensitivity. You do.'

She ignored him. 'And then I did it for the second time. Fell for the most popular, the most charming—'

'I'm not charming,' he cut in. 'And I don't set out to hurt people. Believe me, Kirst, you're the last person in the world I'd want to hurt.' A muscle flickered in his jaw. 'And as for being dumpy and plain and someone to laugh about—have you ever looked in a mirror? I mean, *really* looked?'

She squirmed uncomfortably. 'I wasn't fishing for compliments.'

'I know. And I'm not giving you any. I'm telling you the truth, Kirst. You're lovely.'

Just not lovely enough for him to want to spend the rest of his life with her.

'No wonder you were so angry about our fake engagement,' Ben said softly, surprising her. 'You thought I was spinning a pack of lies, just like him.'

'You were honest with me,' Kirsty said. 'You told me your motives up front.'

'I thought you were safe,' Ben said again. 'Except you weren't.'

And he'd backed off. And she'd left.

'When you went away, everything seemed different,' he continued. 'I can't remember the last time I went out with anyone.'

Oh, really? 'What about Becca?' she gibed.

'Becca?'

'The woman who rang you, the night I got my letter for this job.'

'Becca…' He frowned as if trying to remember. 'Oh. She was a temp at work.'

'She was calling you at home,' Kirsty pointed out tightly.

'Something probably came up on the medical assessment unit.' He shrugged. 'You know how short-staffed we were. I'd agreed to do some extra cover to help out.'

As excuses went, it was a good one. It certainly explained why the woman had been so sure that Ben knew the number—of course he'd know the phone number for the MAU, just as she knew the number for the surgical ward and Theatre. But that tiny corner of doubt remained in Kirsty's mind.

He looked at her. 'Kirst, why are you making such a big deal about it?'

'Because,' she said, 'I'm sick of dealing with your strings of girlfriends.'

'I don't have any strings of girlfriends,' he said.

'Right, and pigs fly.'

'Not any more.' He smiled ruefully at her. 'That's what I'm trying to tell you. I'm a reformed character.'

'Really?' Her voice was heavily laced with sarcasm.

'Yeah. I don't do late nights, I don't do parties and I don't do dates. Oh, and they've changed my name at work. I'm not Dr Charming any more—I'm Dr Grouchy. I go to work, I fix up my patients, I leave. End of story.' He smiled thinly. 'Actually, it's not end of story. And you said I could start in the middle,' he reminded her. 'I go home. Except it isn't home any more—it's the place where I sleep and eat. And even that isn't a brilliant success. Half the time I end up just going down to the beach and staring at the sea until the sun comes up.'

'Must go down a bomb with your housemate.'

'I don't have a housemate.'

She frowned. 'But you advertised for one.'

He shook his head. 'Never got round to it. A couple of people approached me via the grapevine, but I said no. It didn't feel right, having someone in your place.' His blue eyes were very, very serious. 'What I'm trying to say in an incredibly roundabout way is…' His voice cracked. 'I love you, Kirsty.'

Was she dreaming? Or had Ben really said it?

'You…love me?'

'Don't sound so surprised.'

'But…' She stared at him, shaking her head. 'You don't do relationships.'

'I don't know how. That's what I'm asking you, Kirst. Help me.'

'Help you?'

'With the white-lace-and-promises bit. I want to do it—with you.'

'But…we've already told Morag the truth.'

'This isn't about Morag,' he growled. 'It's about us. You and me.'

'We're best friends.'

'You're more than that to me,' he said. 'You're special. I guess I knew that right from the start—right from the first time you sat next to me in a lecture and started chatting to me as if you'd known me all your life.'

'That's what it felt like.'

'I didn't realise just how special you were to me, though, until you walked out.'

'I didn't walk out on you. You drove me up here,' she pointed out.

'Only because you accepted a job up here.'

'Only because I thought you had your usual string of girlfriends and I couldn't just smile and smile and pretend it didn't matter.'

'Kirsty.' Ben drew her hand to his mouth and kissed the tip of each finger in turn. 'Yes, I went out with a few other women. I was panicking, trying to convince myself that I wasn't in love with you.' He smiled wryly. 'It didn't work. Everything reminded me of you and I just didn't know what to do about it. It's taken me way too long to realise it. I know I've hurt you and I don't even know where to start making up for it, but…' He sighed. 'If you tell me to go away and never darken your doorstep again, I'll understand and I'll leave you in peace.'

'And if I don't?'

'Kirsty, will you—? Oh, hell! The drier!'

'Drier?'

He kissed the tip of her nose, set her on her feet and rushed over to the tumble-drier. He turned it off, opened the door and rummaged around inside while Kirsty watched him, faintly bemused.

'This isn't how it was supposed to happen,' he muttered.

'What?'

'It was supposed to be—oh, I dunno—Kew Gardens, the top of the London Eye, somewhere *romantic*.' Not in the middle of Kirsty's tiny kitchen, while he was wearing just a towel! But if he didn't ask her now, he wasn't sure if he'd have the nerve to do it.

He walked back over to her and dropped to one knee. 'Kirsty Brown, will you teach me how to do relationships?'

'Will I…?'

His voice deepened as he opened the warm and soggy box he'd retrieved from his jeans and offered her the ring inside. The same ring he'd given her on the plane. The ring she'd given back to him. 'Marry me, Kirsty.'

Ben—the man who didn't do relationships—was proposing *marriage*!

She looked at him. 'You're in Southbay. I'm here.'

He shrugged. 'No problem. I'll get another job. Even if it means climbing down a rung—you're more important to me than my job.'

'What about children?' she tested.

'I've been thinking about that, too. I know your career's important to you. So I'll stay home with them if you like.'

He'd thought things through *that* far? So there was hope after all. But there was one more barrier they had to cross. 'And your mother?'

His face shuttered. 'She's got nothing to do with this.'

'If she's the reason you back away, then, yes, she has.'

He exhaled sharply. 'Kirst, I don't even know where she is. Even if I did, I'm not sure I want to see her again. I don't want her back in my life just when she pleases. I don't want her to let our children down, the way she let me down.'

'She can't,' Kirsty said simply. 'Because she won't be their parent. We will be.'

'That's not the point.'

'No,' she agreed softly. 'But the point is, Ben—if you can't forgive her for her mistakes, how can you expect anyone else to forgive you for yours?'

'So what are you saying, Kirst? That you won't marry me?'

'I love you, Ben.' This was the hardest thing she'd ever had to do—harder even than walking away from him in Southbay. But, for both their sakes, she had to do it. Slowly, she closed the box and gave it back to him. 'But I don't think you're ready to marry anyone. Not yet.' Not until he'd sorted things out with Sarah.

CHAPTER FIFTEEN

RING the bell. Do it, the voice in Ben's head urged.

But what if...?

Crazy. There was nothing to be frightened about. He dealt with life-and-death situations every day at work, and he had no problems making decisions then. All he had to do was ring the bell.

He nerved himself and did it.

The seconds dragged by. Maybe she was out. Maybe she'd changed her mind. Maybe...

The door opened. Slowly, hesitantly. And a middle-aged woman stood in the doorway, her dark hair streaked with grey and her mouth twisted into a nervous smile.

How long had it been? Fourteen, fifteen years. Just over half his lifetime. He remembered her as taller, thinner, more poised—immaculate make-up and hair. But she was just an ordinary woman.

'Hello.' He couldn't bring himself to call her by her title—but he couldn't be hard enough to use her first name. Not when she was looking even more frightened than he felt.

Her cornflower-blue eyes—so like his own—filled with tears. 'Ben.' Diffidently, she held out her arms.

Ben looked at her. The woman he'd demonised for so long in his head—the woman who'd let him down time after time, until he'd backed away and refused to let her do it again. Kirsty's words echoed in his head. 'If you can't forgive her for her mistakes, how can you expect anyone else to forgive you for yours?'

He stepped forward.

Sarah was shaking as he held her, really shaking. Concerned, he closed the door behind them. 'Where…?' he began.

'Here.' She sniffed as she indicated a door; he guided her through it. 'My boy. I never thought you'd…' Her words dissolved into choking sobs and he settled her down on the sofa next to him.

His eyes widened in surprise as he glanced round the room and saw the framed photographs on the mantelpiece. Himself as a five-year-old in his first school uniform, face full of mischief. As a seven-year-old with a gappy smile after he'd lost his front teeth. As a teenager, grinning broadly as he ripped up his L-plates. A more formal pose in his graduation robes. Another with his white coat on.

But—she hadn't been part of his life. Not at any of those moments.

It was as if she'd read his mind. It was probably written all over his face, he thought wryly as she explained, 'Morag sent them to me.'

He should have guessed. Should have known, the moment Morag had admitted that she'd kept in touch with Sarah over all those years. Because Morag was wise enough and loving enough to do all the things he should have done: to accept Sarah for what she was and make the best of it.

There was a long, long silence.

'Do you want me to, um, get you a glass of water or something?' he asked awkwardly.

She gave him a watery smile. 'She did a good job. She brought you up better than I could have done—she taught you to care about people. I…I'm sorry, Ben. I'm sorry I wasn't a proper mother to you.' She swallowed. 'I missed you. Every second, I missed you. But I couldn't cope, not on my own. I'm weak, Ben. I need someone with me.'

'Gordon.'

She nodded. 'He didn't want kids. It was a straight choice—him or you. I was scared and I was selfish. Ironic, really, that he left me for a woman with three kids.'

'And then it was…' Ben couldn't bring himself to say any more.

She flinched. 'I know. I've been married more times than…more times than was sensible. Apart from your— your dad,' she added shakily, 'I wasn't any good at picking them either.'

'You're married now?'

She shook her head. 'Not for a couple of years. I'm…learning to stand on my own two feet.'

There was a long, long pause. 'I missed you,' she whispered. 'I watched you grow up from a distance. And when you said you'd never see me again…'

'I was fourteen,' he reminded her. 'A stroppy teenager.' The words almost echoed in the air—*and now?*

He could walk away.

Or he could forgive her and move on.

He made his decision. 'I've grown up. And I've come to ask you something.' He fished in his back pocket, retrieved the envelope and handed it to her.

In silence, she opened it—then stared at him. 'You— you want me to come to your wedding?'

He nodded. 'I can't get married without my m—' He stumbled over the word. 'My mother there, can I?'

Crying openly now, Sarah wrapped her arms round him. 'You don't know how much that means to me.'

Ben thought of Kirsty and smiled. Yes, he reflected, he did.

Three months later, Ben was standing at the altar of the small parish church, waiting nervously. The church was packed—the whole village had come to the wedding, plus Kirsty's parents, her brothers and their wives and children, and as many friends and colleagues as could get leave from Kirsty's hospital in London and Jimmy's in Southbay. In the front pews, Sarah and Morag sat together, both misty-eyed. He caught their gaze and smiled.

Trust Kirsty to do things differently. Not for her the

summer wedding in the middle of the day with the sun shining, in the parish church near her parents'. No, she'd wanted to get married in the tiny parish church in Scotland, on a late autumn afternoon, with the church lit by candles and Ben in formal Scots dress—kilt, white dress shirt and a Prince Charlie.

He glanced at his watch. She was late. Please, God. Please, don't let anything have happened to her. Please, don't let her have changed her mind. Please, don't—

And then the organist broke into the first few notes of the Wedding March. Ben just stared and stared as his bride walked down the aisle towards him in her simply cut ivory dress, her eyes shining like gold behind the long ivory veil. Behind her walked Jenny in an equally simply cut dark green dress, Kirsty's two-year-old niece Caitlin in a baby version and her five-year-old twin nephews William and Thomas in child-sized versions of his own outfit.

The ceremony passed in a blur for him. Kirsty actually had to kick him on the ankle to remind him to repeat his vows, but the bits he knew he'd remember all his life were when he gently lifted the veil from her face, when he slipped the plain ring onto her finger and the moment he was allowed to kiss the bride—a moment which went on and on until the vicar gently coughed to remind the groom exactly where he was.

And the reception afterwards was perfect, a traditional Scots meal in the local inn, filled to bursting by the wedding guests, followed by a ceilidh in the village hall. It was while Ben and Kirsty were sitting down, laughing and exhausted after several energetic dances, that he gave her his final wedding present.

'Happy, Dr Robertson?' he asked.

'What do you think?' she teased, her eyes glittering pure gold.

'I think,' he said, 'that I'm going to enjoy this marriage stuff. When we decide where we're going to live, that is.'

The posts Ben had been offered so far meant travelling to the other side of London from Kirsty's flat—a journey almost as long, he'd discovered, as the journey from Southbay to London. But neither of them had wanted to wait any longer before getting married.

'When,' she said wryly.

He fished an envelope from his sporran. 'Mind you, this came in the post this morning. For a Mrs K. Robertson.'

'Mrs?'

'You've passed your exams,' he reminded her. 'So, strictly speaking, you're Mrs now.'

Frowning, Kirsty took the plain brown envelope, slit it open and read it. Her eyes widened. 'They're offering me a consultancy in Southbay.'

'Mmm-hmm.'

'But...' She stared at him. 'Hang on. I've only just opened it. How do you know what it says?'

He fidgeted in his seat. 'I, um, know a couple of people.'

She wrinkled her nose at him. 'You're back to Dr Charming, aren't you?'

'Which makes you Kirsterella,' he shot back.

'Ha, ha. Seriously, Ben—what's this all about?'

He sighed. 'We're not going to tarnish our wedding day with his name, but let's just say that Jimmy's had to replace a certain person.'

'Why?'

He winced. 'A patient—one of your old ones, actually—overheard him propositioning a nurse, then threatening to make sure she lost her job when she turned him down. He complained. There was an inquiry, and a certain SHO decided it was time to speak up.'

'You mean, Paul told them what happened with me?'

He nodded. 'So. They need a replacement. If I go to London, that's two doctors they have to replace. If you come back, their problems are solved.'

'And our accommodation problem,' she added.

'Not to mention that Southbay Infants is listed as a school of excellence.'

Kirsty grinned. 'You're going broody on me.'

He spread his hands. 'I'm being nagged. Gran wants to be a great-gran, and my mother wants to—well, I suppose make up for me by spoiling my children. Your mum overheard them talking, so she cast her vote in favour of babies as well.'

'And what do you want, Ben?' she asked softly.

He smiled. 'You, for the rest of my life.' He kissed her lightly. 'And a little brown-eyed girl to spoil.'

'Blue-eyed boy,' she corrected.

'One of each?'

Kirsty gave him a wicked grin. 'I'll think about it.'

'Just don't keep me in suspense as long as you did when I asked you to marry me,' Ben said, lifting her fingers to his lips and kissing each one slowly. 'Four times, I think it was, before you finally said yes. You even made me put it in writing. And I thought *I* was supposed to be the one with the commitment problem.'

'You were. But you came to your senses.'

'Mmm.' He pulled her close enough so he could whisper in her ear. 'Let's go make babies, Mrs Robertson, super-consultant.'

'Now that, house-husband-to-be,' she whispered back, 'sounds like a very good idea...'

Modern Romance™
...seduction and
passion guaranteed

Tender Romance™
...love affairs that
last a lifetime

Medical Romance™
...medical drama
on the pulse

Historical Romance™
...rich, vivid and
passionate

Sensual Romance™
...sassy, sexy and
seductive

Blaze Romance™
...the temperature's
rising

27 new titles every month.

Live the emotion

MILLS & BOON®

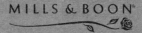

Medical Romance™

TO THE DOCTOR A DAUGHTER by *Marion Lennox*

Dr Nate Ethan has all he needs – a job he loves as a country doctor and a bachelor lifestyle. Dr Gemma Campbell is about to change all that! Her sister has left her with two children – and one of them is Nate's. She must give Nate his baby and walk away – but Nate finds he will do anything to stop her leaving…

A MOTHER'S SPECIAL CARE by *Jessica Matthews*

Dr Mac Grant is struggling as a single dad with a demanding career. Juggling is proving difficult, and he is aware of his son's longing for a mother. Lori Ames is a nurse on Mac's ward – a single mother with a beautiful daughter of her own. Can she bestow upon them the special care that both children so desperately need?

RESCUING DR MACALLISTER by *Sarah Morgan*

A&E nurse Ellie Harrison is intrigued by the ruggedly handsome new doctor at Ambleside. But Dr Ben MacAllister is playing it cool. The pace and excitement of the A&E department thrusts them together and reveals that Ben's growing attraction is as strong as hers – then Ellie realises he has a secret…

On sale 2nd May 2003

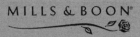

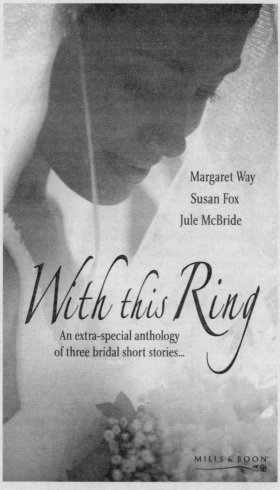

Margaret Way

Susan Fox

Jule McBride

With this Ring

An extra-special anthology
of three bridal short stories...

MILLS & BOON

Available from 18th April 2003

*Available at most branches of WH Smith,
Tesco, Martins, Borders, Eason, Sainsbury's
and all good paperback bookshops.*

0503/024/MB69

2 FREE

books and a surprise gift!

We would like to take this opportunity to thank you for reading this Mills & Boon® book by offering you the chance to take TWO more specially selected titles from the Medical Romance™ series absolutely FREE! We're also making this offer to introduce you to the benefits of the Reader Service™—

    ★ FREE home delivery
    ★ FREE gifts and competitions
    ★ FREE monthly Newsletter
    ★ Exclusive Reader Service discount
    ★ Books available before they're in the shops

Accepting these FREE books and gift places you under no obligation to buy, you may cancel at any time, even after receiving your free shipment. Simply complete your details below and return the entire page to the address below. *You don't even need a stamp!*

YES! Please send me 2 free Medical Romance books and a surprise gift. I understand that unless you hear from me, I will receive 4 superb new titles every month for just £2.60 each, postage and packing free. I am under no obligation to purchase any books and may cancel my subscription at any time. The free books and gift will be mine to keep in any case.

M3ZEA

Ms/Mrs/Miss/Mr ....Initials.....................................
BLOCK CAPITALS PLEASE

Surname ....

Address ....

....

....Postcode.............................

Send this whole page to:
UK: FREEPOST CN81, Croydon, CR9 3WZ
EIRE: PO Box 4546, Kilcock, County Kildare (stamp required)